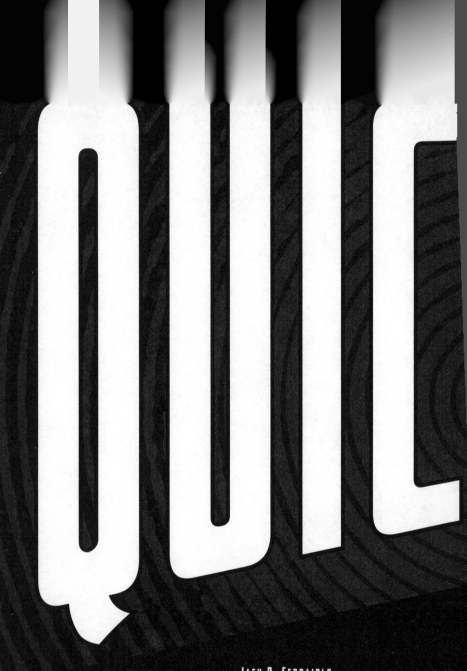

Also by JACK D. FERRAIOLO

The Big Splash

Sidekicks

FIX

By JACK D. FERRAIOLO

Amulet Books

New York

Cataloging-in-Publication Data has been applied for and may be obtained from the Library of Congress.

ISBN: 978-0-8109-9725-7

Text copyright © 2012 Jack D. Ferraiolo
Book design by Chad W. Beckerman

Printed and bound in U.S.A.
10 9 8 7 6 5 4 3 2 1

ABRAMS
THE ART OF BOOKS SINCE 1949

115 West 18th Street
New York, NY 10011
www.abramsbooks.com

To Mom and Dad,
who are probably *still* shocked that
I turned out to be a writer . . .

SOMEONE IS BLACKMAILING VINNY BIGGS —
THE FRANK'S UNDERWORLD
KINGPIN.
WHO WOULD DARE TAKE ON THE BOSS?
MATT STEVENS HAD BETTER FIND OUT
BEFORE HE'S CAUGHT
IN THE CROSSFIRE!

THE SUSPECTS
Kevin Carling, the second-in-command
Will Atkins, the basketball star
Melissa Scott, the loyal girlfriend
Peter Kuhn, the disgraced athlete
Cynthia Shea, the cutthroat cheerleader
Katie Kondo, the hard-as-nails hall monitor
Tim and Tina Thompson, the candy dealers
Or one of a hundred kids who have been
wronged by the Frank's most
ruthless criminal . . .

She stood out from the Monday morning hallway traffic like a gazelle in a herd of cows. She had big blue eyes and blond shoulder-length hair, carefully styled to look carelessly towel-dried. She was thin and athletic, and I'm pretty sure her legs would've kept going if the floor hadn't been there to stop them. She was tapping her right foot, making the light blue miniskirt of her official Franklin Middle School cheerleading uniform bounce in a rhythm that hypnotized every age-appropriate male within four hundred yards. Her name was Melissa Scott. She was as close to a celebrity as you'd find at the Frank, and at the moment, she was leaning against my locker.

"If you're here for my school spirit, you can have it," I said. "I haven't used it in years."

She looked at me as if she couldn't figure out why I was talking to her. Then it dawned on her. "Matt Stevens?" she asked.

"You don't know? I'll try not to take that personally."

She pushed her back off my locker, and I could've sworn I heard the door sigh in disappointment. "You're a detective, right?" she asked in a loud whisper.

"I have my moments."

"I want to hire you."

"Sorry," I said, "but none of my cheers rhyme and I look lousy in a skirt." I opened my locker and put my jacket and bag inside. I was reaching for my first-period books when she grabbed me by the shoulder. She turned me to her and leaned in so that her face was barely an inch away from mine.

"Please," she said in the same loud whisper as before. Her breath smelled like a field of spearmint. She pulled away, scanning the hallway nervously. "I'm sorry I grabbed you."

"Don't be. My social status just jumped a couple of levels."

"I'm so nervous. I don't know what to do . . . He's been acting so—" She stopped herself. "I want to hire you," she repeated.

"Yeah, you mentioned that. For anything in particular?"

"I want you to follow my boyfriend, Will Atkins. He's the captain of the basketball team." As stressed as she was, I could tell she still enjoyed the fact that she could put "my boyfriend," "Will Atkins," and "captain of the basketball team" in the same sentence.

"He's been acting strange lately," she whispered.

"Well, listen . . . I'm touched that you thought of me, but I'm going to have to pass."

"What? Why?"

"I don't take cases that start with 'I want you to follow my boyfriend.' All the paths are rocky and lead to the same place."

She seemed to have no idea what I was talking about.

"I hate to be the one to break this to you," I said, "but there are other pretty girls at the Frank."

She rolled her eyes. "It's not like that."

"Yeah, it never is . . . until it is. And then it's *exactly* like that."

She leveled a gaze at me that I'm pretty sure left scorch marks on the lockers behind me. "You know those girls around here . . . who are sweet and prim and proper? The type of girl who could never, ever even imagine *kissing* a boy?"

"Yeah?"

She smiled and leaned into me, putting her mouth as close to my ear as she could without actually touching it. "Well, I'm the other type."

Her breath tickled, making the hairs on the back of my neck stand on end. She pulled away from me, a high school smile on her seventh-grade face.

"If you say so," I said, trying unsuccessfully to keep my voice from cracking. "So, tell me what you mean by 'acting strangely.' Has he started wearing a gown and high heels to practice? Or is he just having a lot more arguments with his imaginary friend, Reggie?"

"He's been quiet," she answered. "And nervous. And some days it looks like he hasn't slept the night before."

"Maybe he's worried about his crossover dribble. You want my advice? Ask him. Because if you hire me, I can only sneak around so much before *I* eventually ask him. You might as well cut out the middleman and save yourself a couple bucks."

"I did ask him. He said it was nothing."

"Well, there you go. Sounds like he and I agree."

"I'd like to be sure."

"How would you feel if you paid me and I didn't find anything?" I asked.

"I'd feel relieved!" she snipped. "How else would I feel?"

"You'd be surprised how many people want something bad to happen, just so they can feel like they got their money's worth."

"If you don't want the job, I'll find someone else," she said, but she didn't move. As far as bluffs go, it wasn't a very good one.

"I just want you to know what you're getting into," I said. "I don't want to get to the end and have you start haggling over the price."

She laughed as if I'd just insulted her. "You're not exactly going to break my bank."

"Shouldn't you know my rate first before you decide that?"

"Fine. What is it?"

"Two-fifty a day, plus expenses," I said.

She reached into the waistband of her skirt, pulled out a five, and handed it to me. "Is this enough to start?"

I nodded. I meant to say, "I haven't said yes yet," but nothing came out. She was handing me a five-dollar bill that had just been pressed against her stomach. There was no *way* I could speak.

"There's something else," she said. The worry was back on her face. "He dropped by my house yesterday and gave me something to hold. He said he was watching it for a friend and felt that it would be safer with me."

"Why would it be safer with you?"

"He tends to lose things."

"I'll take your word for it. What'd he give you?"

She thought about it for a moment and then said, "I can't tell you."

"We're not off to a great start here."

"He made me promise. It's not his. He's holding it for a friend, and . . . well, he was afraid that if word got around, someone might think it's pretty valuable and try to take it."

"So he gave it to you to hold?" I asked. "Nice guy, setting his girlfriend up to get mugged."

"He said nobody knew he had it, so they'd have no idea that he gave it to me. He also said I was the only one he could trust."

And there it was: the trump card. After that, he could've asked her to walk through walls and she would've been banging into them all day. Now she was hiring me to join her.

"Can you at least give me a hint?" I asked. "Is it something illegal?"

"No, nothing like that! It's just— It's . . . a piece of wood. That's all. No big deal."

"A piece of wood?"

"Yeah, like a decorative—" She stopped herself. "I've already said too much. I'm afraid he's gotten himself involved in something that's way over his head, and this was his way of asking for help."

"I thought you said it was just a piece of wood, that it wasn't a big deal."

"I—I'm not sure what to think anymore," she replied. "That's why I'm hiring you. I used to be friends with Nicole Finnegan, you know. Back in fifth grade. Before she worked for Vinny Biggs . . . I heard what you did for her."

"Which part?" I said. "The part where I inadvertently distracted her so she could get popped with a water cannon, or the part where I did nothing to help her escape the Outs?"

"The part where you solved her case when no one else cared. The part where, despite the fact that she used to be a ruthless criminal, you found justice for her."

If she was aiming for my bull's-eye, she had just hit it, dead-on. "So what would you be hiring me to do?" I asked after a moment's pause. "Follow him or protect you? Because if he *is* in trouble and that piece of wood is in the middle of it, you're the one in the hot seat now."

"I don't care about me. I only care about Will."

"Great. That should make my job easier," I said, and then added, "I need to see it."

"See what?"

"Whatever it is you don't want me to see."

She tensed up, then shifted the backpack on her shoulder. "I . . . uh . . . I don't have it."

"Yes, you do. It's in your bag. No point paying me if you're not going to trust me."

She smiled. Her teeth were perfect, of course. "Okay." She started to pull her backpack around to the front.

I stopped her. "Whoa. Not now. We're starting to draw enough attention as it is. Meet me in the alcove off the gym after lunch."

"I can't. We have a last-minute practice before the game today."

"Okay. Then when?"

"After the game," she said.

"Fine. And bring a friend if you still don't trust me."

"I trust you."

"Yeah, I know," I said. "And it's making me nervous."

If you were taking a bunch of tests to determine whether you felt jealousy or not, tailing Will "Captain of the Basketball Team" Atkins would be the final exam. He was handsome, six inches taller than almost every other kid in school (but not in an awkward, gawky way), and full of the kind of confidence that comes when you're constantly being reminded of how amazing you are. Everyone wanted to be his friend, including the principal and most of the teachers. He was a straight-A student, but I wouldn't fault him if he kept flunking eighth grade on purpose, just so he could stay at the Frank forever.

He was wearing a pair of jeans—the expensive kind that puts its brand name all over the pockets so that you're never at the wrong angle to show people how much you spent on them. The light blue of his official Franklin Middle School basketball jersey (number 4) was the exact same shade as his eyes, making it seem like fate that he was our school's basketball savior.

Today was a game day, so class attendance for Will was encouraged but not really enforced. I could only watch him between classes, as my teachers weren't offering me the same deal. But it didn't matter. Tailing him was as challenging as tailing a school bus on a weekday morning. He couldn't walk two steps without someone coming up to wish him good luck or talk to him about his "plan of attack" for the game that afternoon.

I was looking for any strange or suspicious behavior, but since I had never really watched Will that closely, I had no idea what was strange for him. I was hoping for something obvious, like a sudden screaming fit, but no such luck.

For a kid who could get away with whatever he wanted, Will was modest and approachable. He talked to *everyone*, regardless of their social status. In fact, he seemed to enjoy his conversations with geeks and nerds the most. He looked everyone in the eye as they spoke to him. He nodded and smiled, but in a way that indicated that he wasn't just glad-handing; he was actually listening. His laugh was easy and genuine. And you could tell when someone paid him a compliment, because he'd turn bright red and look at his shoes. It appeared that the only person who didn't buy into the hype of "Will the Legend" was Will himself.

That's not to say he didn't have his share of quirky habits. As soon as he'd start walking, he'd start whistling, as if there was no way to do one without doing the other. It was always the same tune, something that sounded like a cross between "Happy Birthday" and "Mary Had a Little Lamb." Sometimes, when he was standing around, he'd hum it to himself, like a pep talk or a quiet prayer. He tapped his teeth when he was thinking, and snapped his fingers when he was restless . . . which was a lot of the time. Before he opened his locker, he'd knock on the door four times—the same number that was on the back of his jersey.

None of this seemed suspicious to me. Quirky and superstitious, perhaps, but not suspicious. I've met a lot of athletes in my time, and all of them were superstitious in one way or another. I once played baseball with a kid who would tap the plate the same number of times as his jersey number. A couple of years ago, he wore the number 48. After a few twenty-minute at-bats, the coach made him switch to number 3. Everyone agreed it was the right thing to do.

When lunch finally came, the only things I'd discovered about Will was that he was apparently one of the nicest kids in school and also that he was a pretty decent whistler. I also realized that I should've started watching him last year. It might've inspired me to play basketball, which seemed to drastically change the whole middle school experience. He definitely looked like he was having more fun than I was.

By the time I entered the caf, lunch was already in full swing. I used some of my advance to buy whatever they were substituting for food that day, then found a seat two tables over from Melissa Scott.

She and her friends were at their regular table, the top of which was covered with more makeup than food. She was trying to act casual, but I sensed that her responses to her friends were forced, and her laughs were a few seconds late. She scanned the cafeteria. When she finally found me, she shot a clear "Well, what did you find out?" look my way. I returned it with a half-smile and a noncommittal headshake as if to say, "Not much." Before she could volley back, a hulking eighth grader stepped into my sight line. I looked up at him and smiled. He smiled back. Another huge kid came up beside me and put a hand the size of a bear paw on my shoulder. "Mr. Biggs wants to talk to you," he said in a surprisingly high, clear voice.

"I'm honored," I said. "What are the topics today? Renewable energy sources? The European economy? My favorite kind of pie?"

The kid in front of me grabbed my tray. "You finished with this?" he asked as he slid it off the end of the table. It landed with a crash, spraying ground beef and mystery sauce all over the floor.

"You know," I said, "I get the feeling you didn't actually care whether I was finished or not."

The kid behind me lifted me out of my seat. "Time to go."

"Well, now you're just being rude," I told him.

He carried me through the cafeteria like a bag of garbage he was lugging to the sidewalk. No one looked over; they just kept going about their business.

Vincent Biggio, a.k.a. Vinny Biggs, was the seventh-grade head of a criminal operation that controlled most of the illegal activities here in the Frank. He was sitting at a table in the corner with his back to the wall. You'd need a sledgehammer to sneak up on him. He was eating a plate of spaghetti so delicious-looking, I didn't even need to check the cafeteria menu to know that he hadn't gotten it there.

The kid who was carrying me placed me back onto the floor, more gently than I expected. The other kid pulled the chair that was opposite Vinny out from under the table. He made an elegant gesture for me to sit down. I did. Vinny ignored me and brought a forkful of perfectly wound spaghetti up to his pudgy face. He chewed slowly, looking out over the caf as if he couldn't see me sitting in front of him, like a farsighted king looking out over a courtyard full of subjects. He dabbed the corners of his mouth with a linen napkin.

Sitting to Vinny's left was his right-hand man, Kevin Carling. Kevin's roast beef sandwich sat in front of him, untouched. He was watching me with an expression I couldn't read, which was unusual. Before he got tangled up with Vinny, Kevin was my best friend. I thought I had all of his expressions memorized and cataloged.

A few weeks ago, Kevin had made it clear to me that he was going to try to leave Vinny's organization. Yet here he was, still performing the duties of a loyal second in command. If he *was* going to leave, he sure was taking the scenic route.

I leaned back in the chair and folded my arms. I stared at Vinny, my jaw tight, my expression blank but with a hint of contempt. "You owe me two bucks for the lunch your meatheads trashed," I said.

"If you bought it here, they did you a favor."

"Probably . . . but I had almost figured out what it was. Now the suspense is going to kill me."

Vinny snapped his fingers. Two dollar bills appeared on the table in front of me. I picked them up, folded them, and put them in my shirt pocket. "Thanks," I said. I started to stand up, but a giant hand on my shoulder guided me back down, gently but firmly. I sighed.

"I am about to offer you a job," Vinny said.

"Let me save us both a little time," I replied. "No."

"You should hear the offer first."

"What's to hear? You're going to tell me that you'll pay me a ridiculous amount of money to do some 'easy' job that we both know isn't really easy. Do you think I forgot what happened two weeks ago?"

Vinny smiled. "No. I just assumed you raised your

rates." He gave a quick look to the kid standing over my right shoulder, and a second later, a stack of five-dollar bills appeared on the table. I looked down at the money for a moment, then back at Vinny.

"You won't even touch them," he said, laughing. "I would be insulted, except this is the very reason I'm hiring you." He reached over and pulled the stack closer to the middle of the table, then fanned the bills out. There were eight of them. I counted them four times to make sure.

When I looked at Vinny, he was smiling at me. "That's just to start," he said. "There are eight more when you complete the job."

I glanced at Kevin, but his expression was still unreadable. I looked back at Vinny. "You're crazy," I said. "Either that or you think I am."

"On the contrary. I think I know when to pay top dollar to get the job done right."

"Or when to pay extra for just the right kind of sucker."

"Matthew, you and I both know that you're nobody's sucker." I started to speak, but he cut me off. "And if you insist on bringing up events from a couple of weeks ago, may I remind you that *you* are sitting here in front of me, safe and sound, while others are not."

"And you're looking to change that?"

"Please. I'm not in the habit of spending forty dollars on something I can get done for less." He stared at me for an extra beat to remind me that this was not an exaggeration or a cheap threat, just the simple truth. "But let's forget all that," he said with a casual wave of his hand. "Our previous 'disagreement' was just business, Matthew. At least, for me it was. It certainly doesn't alter my opinion of you."

"Which is . . ."

"That you are one of the few people in this hovel who stood up for me when I was nobody." He paused for a moment. "Less than nobody," he amended.

"Yeah, you've tried this tactic before, remember?"

"It's not a tactic, Matthew. It's the truth. You are a rare breed in the Frank," he said. "You have integrity."

"Paying for integrity. Novel concept."

"Anyway, either you're in business or you're not," he said. "If you are, then I wish to hire you. Do you want to know what for?"

"Does it matter?"

He smiled in a way that indicated that it didn't. "There's a piece of wood that's gone missing. It's about this big." He held his hands up, indicating that the four-inch space between them was the size of the wood. It was about the size of a piece of white bread. "It has a design carved into one side of it. Not a picture or anything. Just some decorative swirls."

"A decorative piece of wood," I said, trying to keep my face and voice as even as possible.

"Yes. As I've said, it's gone missing, and I want it back."

"Was it yours to begin with?" I asked.

"Of course."

We stared at each other for a minute. He knew I didn't believe him, and I knew he didn't care what I believed.

"You have until Friday," he said. He pushed the stack of fives closer to me.

I didn't touch them. "That sounds like a threat."

"Think of it more as an expiration date."

"For me or the job?"

"Whatever motivates you, Matthew." He paused. "Now, if you'll excuse me . . ."

One of the big kids picked me up again, but I wasn't in the mood. I squirmed and jerked away, breaking his grip. He smiled at me and held his hands up in an "Okay, I won't touch you" kind of way. As I was watching him, the other goon must've picked the forty dollars up off the table, because before I could react, he was shoving the bills into my shirt pocket. He slapped my chest once, to make sure the money stuck. It stuck, all right. It was practically embedded.

Vinny was back to eating his spaghetti and pretending like I was made of clear plastic. Kevin had started to eat his sandwich, but he kept his eyes on me.

I turned and walked away. I looked over at Melissa's table, but she and her friends were gone.

I headed toward the exit, trying to move quickly without being noticed. Finding Melissa without looking like I was trying to find Melissa was my new number-one priority. Vinny didn't know that she had what he was looking for, but I knew it wouldn't be long before he did. The hallways of the Frank have eyes and ears, and one way or another, they all belonged to him.

$\mathcal{I}$ was willing to bet most of my birthday money that the "decorative piece of wood" Vinny had just hired me to find was the same "decorative piece of wood" that Melissa's boyfriend had given her to hold. This was a middle school, not a flea market . . . there weren't a lot of fancy knickknacks floating around here.

I had to talk to Melissa and let her know that the status of her case had changed from "somewhat concerning" to "watch your butt" faster than you could say "Go, team, go!" I had three classes to get through before the game started, and only a couple of minutes between each to try to talk to her. And I had to be careful. My social rank wasn't high enough that I could just walk up to a cheerleader and start talking to her. Our chat this morning was a news item that might still be making the rounds; if we added an afternoon talk, we might start a full-blown rumor. And that might be just enough to make Vinny suspicious.

I shouldn't have worried so much. Talking to a cheerleader one-on-one on a game day was impossible. The few times I saw her in the hallway, she was surrounded by other cheerleaders. The best I could do was give her a few vaguely ominous facial expressions. She even tried to stop once, but the flock around her was in perpetual motion, all fluttering skirts and chirpy chatter, urging her along.

When I wasn't trying to get Melissa's attention, I was trying to sort out the particulars of my plan. The first course of action I was going to suggest was that she give the piece of wood back to Will. It was nice that she wanted to help him, but she wasn't seeing the full picture. Vinny wanted that piece of wood, and he would have no qualms about putting her in the Outs to get it.

I didn't know how it worked in other middle schools, but life here in the Frank was pretty cheap. It didn't take much—just a splash of liquid below the belt—and you'd find yourself in the Outs, the least popular "club" in school. Then, for all intents and purposes, your life was over.

Vinny had started the Outs last year. It was the last key step in his rise to power.

Once, Vinny was nothing more than a victim of ridicule, another chubby kid whose only seeming purpose was to be a whipping boy for the big, the mean, and the popular. Nobody bothered to find out if he was capable of anything more than absorbing abuse.

It turned out that he was capable of a lot more.

Vinny started building his organization right under everyone's noses. He found kids with angelic faces and devilish attitudes, then paid them handsomely to steal answer keys to exams. It was a smart investment, and he used some of the earnings to branch out.

He used his own weight issues to become the poster child for anti-obesity, convincing the administration that the sweets available in the school cafeteria had contributed to his weight gain. It worked. The vending machines got moved out, but everyone's desire for junk food stayed put. And guess who was there to fill the void? Yep— Vinny. He had funneled some of his stolen-exam money into buying oversized bundles of candy from one of those wholesale clubs. He slapped APPROVED stickers on them, then hired some eighth-grade muscle to make sure that his was the only candy in the Frank. The result? Another fortune.

Vinny's organization kept getting bigger, but also harder for him to handle on his own. He came to me, asking if I wanted to become his second in command . . . mostly because when he was still getting picked on, I had gone out of my way to stand up for him. I turned him down. I saw where he was heading, and I didn't like it.

My best friend, Kevin, had a different opinion . . . and when Vinny went to him with the same offer, Kevin said yes.

It killed our friendship.

With Kevin at his side, Vinny dipped his fingers into forgeries. If you needed a doctor's note or a hall pass or even a whole report card, Vinny supplied it, and at a reasonable price. Then he really got serious: gambling.

Kevin and Vinny set up books on all of the school's sports teams. Gambling exploded, doubling Vinny's "earnings" almost overnight. The only problem he encountered was that some kids still viewed him as a pudgy little punching bag. Those bullies would convince him to front them the money for their bets. Then, when they lost, they'd refuse to pay up.

Vinny had to make an example of them; otherwise his whole business would collapse. Beating kids up would draw the attention of adults. Plus, it might inspire some of the tougher kids to group together and fight back. No . . . he had to find a way to humiliate kids, knock them completely off the social board. That's where the Outs came in.

He started by targeting kids who had tormented him in the past. He had his hit kids squirt the victims in the front of their pants, to make it look like they had peed themselves. If you got marked with the pee stain, you'd find yourself instantly surrounded by a jeering crowd determined to destroy your reputation and your self-respect.

Was it childish? Sure. Did most kids know the pee was fake? Yeah, probably. But it didn't matter. Once a kid got marked, the rest of the school would gang up and make his—or her—life miserable. Whether the pee was fake or not wasn't the point. The real point was that, in a lot of ways, middle school was rotten. Most kids felt like they were one false move away from becoming the class joke anyway—one little slipup, and they'd become a laughingstock. That's what Vinny counted on. He turned that fear into a weapon. If everyone was laughing at someone else, that meant that they weren't laughing at you.

Once you were in the Outs, you were done for. You were an outcast. As far as everyone else was concerned, you didn't exist anymore. Kids in the Outs were ghosts of their former selves, completely invisible—unless someone needed a whipping post . . . Then they were automatically elected.

Kids in the Outs came in all shapes and flavors: ordinary kids who got themselves in over their heads with candy or gambling debts; populars who thought their status allowed them to get away with anything; former employees of Vinny's who got a little greedy. No one was untouchable. There was no such thing as being too good or too tough or too popular. If you got splashed, you were in the Outs. End of story.

I'd thought about trying to stop it—trying to turn the tide, trying to get everyone to stop buying into this whole stupid system. But I was just one kid. Greater forces than I wanted this system in place. If I tried to put a stop to it, I'd find myself up "Pee-Pee River" without a paddle, and then I'd be no use to anyone. The best I could do was to work with people who needed help but couldn't figure out where to get it. And once I found them (or they found me), I did all I could to protect them.

And that's why, even though this case had grown into something a lot bigger and more dangerous than I had expected, I was sticking by Melissa. She was in trouble, and she'd hired me to help her. The size of the trouble may have changed, but that only meant she needed me more— even if she would never admit it. Cheerleaders were higher up on the social ladder, but they weren't immune to the Outs. In fact, when it happened, they fell harder than others. I knew that if Melissa was stubborn enough to hold on to that piece of wood, she didn't stand a chance. Giving it back to Will might be her best shot, because he might be the only kid in the entire school who couldn't be put in the Outs.

Why? Because he was in a social class all his own. Kids in the Frank worshipped him, not only for his looks and his ability on the court (although that was part of it) but also for his integrity. Everyone loved him. He could be the only kid in school that the other kids wouldn't rush to humiliate, and Vinny knew it. If Melissa gave Will the piece of wood and Vinny tried to put Will in the Outs, it might not stick. Then the whole fragile house of cards could come tumbling down . . . and take Vinny's entire organization with it.

When the bell finally rang for my last class of the day, I ran out the door. If I made it down to the gym before the game started, there was a chance I could talk to Melissa alone. I might even be able to take some of the heat off her—

He came out of nowhere, or at least it seemed that way because I wasn't paying attention. In half a second, my back was against a row of lockers, and a pale white forearm was pressing into my neck. A matching pale, greasy face was staring at me, mouth in a twisted sneer, showing just a glimpse of yellow teeth. A ragged black line from the dye in his hair bled onto his forehead.

"Timothy Thompson," I said. "You handsome devil! When's your book on beauty tips coming out?"

His sneer widened, showing a little more of his corn-colored teeth, but he didn't say anything.

His sister, Tina Thompson, came sauntering toward me. "Matthew Stevens," she said, dragging out every syllable.

Tim and Tina were fraternal twins who were sure that nature had made a mistake by not making them identical, so they tried to correct it. They wore the same clothes and the same shoes, and had the same black hair (his was dyed), cut in the same short, head-hugging manner. If it wasn't for the fact that they looked nothing alike, you wouldn't be able to tell them apart. They were twice as creepy as they looked and four times as shady.

In some ways, they were like me: kids who didn't have any allegiance to any group. The difference was that I liked to think I had some morals . . . maybe even a little bit of honor. The Thompsons were ruthless. They wanted money, and a lot of it. And they didn't give a damn how they got it.

"Tina," I said. "Tell your brother he can hug me all he wants, but pretty soon I'm going to start charging him."

"I think he heard you just fine," she said. Tim squeezed my throat a little to show me that he had. "We have a job offer for you," she continued, "and we want to make sure we have your attention."

"Do you always rough up your potential employees?" I asked.

She stopped to think. "You know, we've never had employ*ees* before . . . only employ*ers*. You treat people so much better when they give you money, don't you think?"

"Are we going someplace specific," I asked, "or are we

just going to wander around all day, waiting for one of you to say something witty?"

Tina looked at me. Her face was twitching. It took me a minute to realize that she was trying to look sad. "We lost something," she finally said. "And we'd like you to find it for us."

"If it's your individual identities, I think you're out of luck. Nobody's seen those in years."

Tim squeezed my throat again. I thought about biting his arm, but I didn't want to risk catching any diseases. His sister put her hand up. Tim loosened his grip.

"It's a piece of wood with a pretty design carved into it," Tina said.

I clenched my jaw and tried not to blink.

"Our grandfather gave it to us," she continued. "Right before he died, and . . . well, we do miss him so." She started to cry, but apparently her tears were the kind that evaporated on contact with oxygen. "We can't understand why anyone would want to take it from us, seeing as it has absolutely no value except for sentimental." Her breath hitched, and she cut off the flow of invisible tears.

"Someone took it from you?" I asked. "I thought you said it was lost."

"It is. We suspect it may have been stolen, though."

"What makes you suspect that?"

She looked at her brother, who gave her a subtle headshake. "I really don't feel comfortable talking about it until we have an agreement," she said. "Will you help us, Matt? Please?" She tried to make a sympathetic face, but all she could muster was one of hunger and desperation, with a little bit of disgust for having said the word "please."

"Sorry. I'm in the middle of a couple of things right now." I reached up and grabbed Tim's forearm with both hands, then twisted my hands in opposite directions. "Rope burn!" I yelled, apparently unable to contain myself.

"Gah!" he shouted, and let go of me. I took hold of the front of his shirt with my left hand, and cocked my right in the ready position. His eyes went wide, anticipating impact.

Then I heard the squirt gun click in front of me. It sounded like a big one. I looked up. It was.

"Thank you for your time, Matt," Tina said. "Come along, Tim."

I let go of Tim's shirt, giving him a little push as a good-bye. He gave me a sneer for the road, then walked toward his sister. Tina pulled a couple of thin, brightly colored objects out of her back pocket. She tossed them to me; they landed at my feet. They looked like straws in homemade wrappers. "If you happen to come across our memento," she said, "reward is in the *triple* digits."

She held out her arm. Tim took it. They walked off without looking back.

I waited until they had disappeared before I bent down and picked up the straws at my feet. They were Pixy Stix . . . containing the Thompsons' own special blend. There was a phone number printed on the side of the wrapper.

I tore one open, dabbed my pinkie finger into the powder, then put the powder onto my tongue. My head almost exploded. It was pure sugar, but with hints of watermelon, strawberry, and bubblegum. It was easy to see how someone could get addicted.

I threw the opened straw in the trash, then put the unopened one in my pocket and started running toward the gym. I had to get to Melissa.

The girl who answered the practice room door
stared at me with a look that was teetering between
curiosity and annoyance. Her name was Cynthia Shea,
and she was the head cheerleader. "May I help you?" she
asked at last.

Behind her, I could hear the sounds of cheerleaders
warming up. I tried to get a glimpse of Melissa, but
Cynthia had only opened the door wide enough for her
face to peek out.

It was a flawless face. Dark and smooth, it was the
kind of face you could stare at for hours, even if it meant

you'd be labeled "the creepy kid who stares at girls' faces for hours." Her curly black hair was pulled through an elastic that looked overmatched. I knew how it felt.

"I need to talk to Melissa Scott," I said.

Her smile was stiff and polite. "I'm sorry. We're a little busy right now. You can talk to her—"

"It's important."

Her eyes narrowed to slits. "Lots of things are important," she said.

I waited for her to say something else, but she didn't.

"I need to talk to her," I said. "It'll only take a minute."

"Okay, listen . . ." She paused so that I could fill in my name.

"Matt," I said, as my ego took one on the chin.

"Matt," she repeated. "We don't have a minute. The game starts in five, and we need—"

"Look, forget your stupid game!" I yelled, then immediately regretted it. The volume of the practice sounds behind Cynthia took a noticeable dip. The last thing I wanted to do was to draw attention to myself or the fact that I was trying to get in contact with Melissa. So what had I done? I had yelled at the head cheerleader and caused a scene in front of the entire squad. The smooooooth Matt Stevens strikes again.

A cheerleader came trotting up behind Cynthia. "You okay, Cyn?"

"Yeah, I've got this. Go run them through the opening routine."

"Got it." The cheerleader flitted off to her assignment. Cynthia stepped out into the hallway and closed the door behind her. "Listen . . . Matt," she said, the annoyance in her voice unmistakable. "I'm sure you believe that whatever it is that you're worked up about is justification for you to yell at me, but I assure you that it isn't."

"Sorry. Honestly. But I really need to talk to Melissa. Now."

"I don't think you're hearing me, Matt. That's not going to happen."

She was drawing a line in the sand, and in order for me to cross it, I was going to have to give up more information than I was comfortable with. I took a deep sigh. "Are you practicing right up to game time?"

"Yes. If you need to talk to her so badly, she'll have some free time a little after tip-off."

That might be too late, I thought, but didn't say it. I sighed again. "Fine." I started to walk away.

"What's this about?" she called after me.

"I just bought a new pair of pom-poms, but I can't get

them to work," I said, and walked away without waiting for her response.

When I entered the gym, both teams were in their layup lines. The bleachers were already full of kids anxious to cheer Will on to victory.

Even though the team had crashed and burned last year, there was a sense of optimism leading into this season, and almost all of that optimism was centered around Will. He was always the best player on the court, regardless of who the other team was. But there was something else, something beyond his athletic ability that made kids want to show up and support him: He loved the game. It was obvious from the way he played. And he had proved that no matter how much the odds were stacked against him, he would never stop giving his all. Even if his own teammates were clearly on the take, doing everything they could to prevent the team from winning, it didn't matter . . . He would *never* stop fighting. That kind of determination gave kids hope, and hope in the Frank was rare.

I walked into the gym, scanning the crowd for any sign of Vinny or the Thompsons. Instead, I spotted Liz

Carling. She was sitting at the end of the bleachers, fifth row up from the court. Her foot was dangling off the side. I walked over and stood below her, her foot even with my face. She smiled. "Matt," she said. "I didn't know you liked basketball."

"Doesn't everyone at the Frank?"

"Apparently," she said, looking at the full bleachers. "I could scoot over if you want to sit down."

I shook my head no, even though there was nothing I wanted more than to sit down next to Liz and forget about everything other than the fact that I was sitting next to Liz. She was Kevin Carling's younger sister, a year behind Kevin and me, but that never mattered. Liz was smarter and savvier than most of the teachers.

Her hair was so black that it was almost blue, and it was cut in a boyish bob that framed her face perfectly. She was wearing a dark purple velvet dress that managed to look fancy and casual at the same time, with black tights and black shoes. She was so cute that you might underestimate her, and that would be your downfall. Liz was a world-ranked chess player. You took her lightly at your own risk.

She and I had been friends forever, but lately our

relationship had drifted into new territory. We'd held hands—and each other—in a way that felt outside the boundaries of "regular" friendship. I had certainly never done either of those things with any of my other friends.

What did it mean? I had no idea, and I liked to think that she didn't, either . . . but I could never be sure. I always got the feeling that Liz knew something I didn't.

"You're on a job," she said, this time giving me a quick glance.

"Is it that obvious?"

"Do you want the honest answer or the lying-but-supportive answer?"

"Your choice."

"Okay . . . No! It is not obvious that you are on a job," she said with fake stiffness.

"Thanks," I said sarcastically.

"Anytime. No, really." She paused for dramatic effect. "Anytime."

The teams were huddling at their respective benches, getting last-second instructions. Will was looking at the coach with an expression of intense focus, as if the coach was revealing the secrets of the universe on his miniature dry-erase board.

The cheerleaders were performing on the sidelines.

They were in two rows, one behind the other. Melissa was in the front row, dead center. She was running through the routine with her eyes closed. Right before the end of the cheer, she opened them, and our eyes locked. She immediately stopped what she was doing and almost got a leg kick in the face from the girl next to her. Cynthia walked over to Melissa and started to give her an earful, but she didn't seem to be listening; her eyes stayed focused on me.

"Melissa Scott is staring at you," Liz said.

"Is she?"

"Should I be worried?"

I shook my head but didn't say anything.

"Can you talk about it?" she asked, still looking straight ahead.

"Not right now."

"Anything I can do to help?"

I shook my head again, but it was a slow shake, with a small hitch. To be honest, I wasn't sure if she could help or not; I was just saying no out of habit.

Liz didn't ask for an explanation. She dropped her hand over the side of the bleachers. I reached up and took it. She grabbed hold and squeezed, running her thumb over the back of my hand. My heart and stomach flopped at the same time, making it feel like they were trying to switch places inside me. She let go of my hand.

I nodded my head at Melissa, then held my hand to my chest, and gave what I hoped was a subtle finger point toward my left, her right. There was an exit door near her, and another near me. Both led to the same hallway. Melissa gave a little nod and said something to Cynthia. Cynthia didn't look happy about it and waved her hand dismissively. Melissa started for her exit door. I waited a moment before heading toward mine.

"Be careful," Liz said.

"Careful's never helped me."

"Then be reckless, but good." She turned toward me at last and winked.

I had taken three steps toward the exit when the scream came.

Everything in the gym stopped. I started running, crashing through the exit door.

Melissa was on the hallway floor. She was crying, hysterical. Her backpack was lying next to her, torn. The contents were spread all around her. There was a giant wet spot on the front of her skirt.

"Melissa!" I yelled, running toward her. "Melissa!"

"He took it! He took it!" she screamed. She was looking past me as if I wasn't even there.

"We have to get you out of here." I started to grab her arm and pick her up, but she was dead weight. "Melissa! Stand up!"

Kids were streaming into the hallway behind me, running to see the source of the screaming.

"Melissa!" I yelled.

"He took it!" she yelled.

"It doesn't matter! You have to—"

It was too late.

"Melissa peed herself!" someone shouted. The laughter started almost immediately, multiplying exponentially until it filled the entire hallway. "PEE-PEE PANTS! PEE-PEE PANTS!" the crowd chanted as it surged forward like a conquering army. Melissa was just lying there, sobbing, picking up her stuff from the floor, then putting it down again, hoping the piece of wood was still there.

"PEE-PEE PANTS! PEE-PEE PANTS!"

"Forget the piece of wood and get out of here!" I yelled at Melissa, but I don't think she heard me. She didn't move.

The crowd kept coming. The only thing standing between all those kids and Melissa was me. I turned to face them, but I felt like a mouse about to face a mob of hungry cats.

"PEE-PEE PANTS! PEE-PEE PANTS!"

"Leave her alone!" came an authoritative shout from the back. The kids in the rear stopped and turned; some of the curiosity traveled as far up as the midpoint of the crowd. The kids in the front paid no attention to it, though, and continued to push forward.

"PEE-PEE PANTS! PEE-PEE PANTS!"

"I said, leave her alone!" The voice was closer now, moving up through the crowd. I craned my neck to see. It was Cynthia. There were two cheerleaders flanking her. She was pushing people out of the way. Some of the kids were letting her, but I suspect that it was just so they could brag later that she touched them.

I was still holding Melissa's arm when Cynthia got to me. She grabbed the front of my shirt and held it tight. "Get your hands off of her!" she shouted.

"I'm trying to help her!" I yelled back, but she didn't seem to hear me.

While Cynthia was holding on to my shirt, Melissa tried to stand up, but the floor was wet. Her foot slipped, and she went back down with a plop. Whatever quiet

Cynthia had fought for was gone. The crowd started surging forward again, laughing and chanting.

"PEE-PEE PANTS! PEE-PEE PANTS!"

"Stop it!" Cynthia yelled. I don't think they were listening anymore. "STOP IT!"

She had lost her bid for control. And because she was still holding on to the front of my shirt, she was preventing *me* from doing anything. I grabbed her wrist and twisted it, just enough to break her grip. She let out a yelp.

I pushed her out of the way, then turned to Melissa. She was still sitting in the puddle, not even trying to get up anymore. Some weaselly looking kid was yelling in her face, his nose about an inch away from hers. I put my hand in between them, then grabbed the kid's weasel face and shoved him into the crowd.

I lifted Melissa up and started guiding her away. "Run," I said. She looked at me, her eyes wide with shock, her teeth chattering as if the temperature in the hallway had suddenly plummeted. "RUN!" I shouted into her face, then turned her away from the crowd and gave her a gentle push to get her started. Her legs were unsteady, but they held. She built up a little momentum and started to run.

The crowd tried to follow her. Weasel-face was out in front again, laughing and chanting. I tripped him. He went down, face-first, smacking his palms onto the floor. I grabbed the runty kid that was behind him, spun him around, and flung him into the crowd, causing a domino effect that knocked over the front line and slowed the rushing mob. By the time they had recovered, Melissa was gone. Cynthia broke through and ran down the hall after her.

The crowd started to disperse, filtering back into the gym. The weasel-face kid stood up and got in my face. "What is your problem?!?"

I was about to shove my hand through his chest when Liz came over. "Hey!" she yelled. He turned toward her. She grabbed his shirt and slammed him into the wall.

"Who the hell are you?" he yelled.

"I'm the girl who's about to embarrass you more than you've already embarrassed yourself."

He looked at me. "Whatsa matter, tough guy? Need a girl to fight your—"

Liz punched him in the arm. Hard.

"Ahhhh! Hey!" he yelled, rubbing his shoulder.

"No, he doesn't *need* me to," she said. "I just like to. Now beat it."

The kid started to say something but then stopped. He looked from Liz to me, then back to Liz. He must've seen that we weren't happy, and that hitting him was at the top of our "This Will Make Us Feel Better" list, because he kept his mouth shut and walked away. When he was well out of punching range, he turned and yelled, "Jerks!"

"So . . . that thing you're working on . . . Can you talk about it now?" Liz asked.

I shook my head. "This has gotten way too hot way too fast," I said. "*I* don't want to be involved, let alone drag you into it." That made me think about Will and Melissa. That's exactly what he had done: dragged her into his mess . . . or set her up. Either way, it didn't paint a very flattering picture of Will "Savior of Franklin Middle School" Atkins.

I picked up Melissa's bag. It had a pink and yellow argyle pattern on it. One of the straps was ripped. The front flapped open like a torn piece of skin. There were still a couple of pens and some makeup inside—and a couple of straws, wrapped up in brightly colored, homemade wrappers. I took one out. There was a phone number printed neatly on the side. The same number that was on the straw that Tina Thompson had tossed to me earlier. I dropped the straw back in the bag.

Liz picked up the rest of Melissa's stuff from the floor and handed it to me. I put it back inside the bag, then zipped it up. There were three or four drops of black ink or dye on the outside of the bag. I checked the floor. A few similar-looking drops were there as well.

"Found something?" Liz asked.

"Yeah. Go home, Liz," I said. "Right now. And watch out."

"For what?"

"Twins."

$\mathcal{M}ost$ of the kids who had yelled at and humili-
ated Melissa marched right back into the gymnasium to
resume rooting for the basketball team. The idea that
it might be ridiculous for them to have "school spirit"
minutes after totally crushing the spirit of one of their
classmates—a cheerleader, no less—seemed lost on them.

Some other kids—too hopped up from all the excitement—decided that they couldn't sit still, even for a
basketball game, so they wandered the hallways, talking
loudly with other jittery kids. Some lamented the fact
that the school was going to hell in a handbasket; others

talked about how "awesome" the takedown had been and wondered out loud what Melissa had done to deserve her fate. Maybe the kid who took her out was a girl who got cut from the cheerleading squad. Or maybe it was a girl who had the hots for Will and wanted Melissa out of the picture. Or maybe Melissa had been seeing another boy on the side, behind Will's back, and the other boy decided that if he couldn't have her all to himself, then nobody else could have her, either.

I started walking faster, trying hard to tune out the chatter. I had already chosen an outlet for my anger, and I didn't want to waste any of it on these kids.

Both the Thompsons were standing in front of Tim's open locker. They looked giddy, laughing and talking as if they had just aced a final. A couple of kids approached them and exchanged some money for a few of their special Pixy Stix. The four of them smiled and laughed. It looked like the Thompsons' joy was infectious . . . and came in brightly colored wrappers.

I was fifteen feet away when Tim turned in my direction. He must have been expecting me, because he gave me a smug smile. I walked right up to him, put my hand around his neck, and shoved him against his neighbor's locker. His smile remained, but I had knocked some of the smugness out of it.

"Well . . . aren't you two a scummy little family," I said.

"Let go of me," Tim snarled.

"You talk?" I asked. "I thought you were the 'silent, creepy type.'"

"Oh, Matty-boy!" came Tina's singsongy voice from behind me. I didn't even have to look. I could hear her pumping the squirt gun. I wheeled around, using Tim as a shield. I had one of his arms bent back at a painful angle. It was a soaker, and Tina held it with steady hands. Tim was shaking with fury. Kids around us were starting to take an interest while trying hard to look like they weren't.

"Is there something we can help you with?" Tina asked, as if she was standing behind a counter, offering to sell me something.

"I want the piece of wood," I said. "The one you stole from Melissa right before you put her in the Outs."

"I'm sorry," she said with mock innocence, "but I have no idea what you're talking about."

"Really?" I asked, torquing Tim's arm a little. He yelped. "Any ideas now?"

"Ohhhh . . . ," she said as if her memory had just kicked in. "You mean our great-aunt's memento."

"Right—except on the first go around it was your grandfather's."

"We have so many loving relatives, it's hard to keep them all straight."

"Yeah, especially when half of them don't exist," I said. "Now, where is it?"

She smiled, but it looked like it was hurting her. "Do you have a plan for the next step," she asked, "or are we going to stay like this until the end of the day?"

"Sure, I've got a plan. First, you're going to drop the squirt gun. Second, I'm going to search your brother's locker for the item you stole from Melissa. Third, if I don't find it in his locker, you're going to tell me where I *can* find it, or I'm going to break Tim in half and use the pieces to knock you around. Got it?"

"Ooh, that does sound frightening," she said. "Doesn't that sound frightening, Tim?"

Tim snarled. "Let go of me!" He started to squirm more violently, but I managed to keep a hold. Everyone was watching us now. They started to creep forward.

"What Tim is trying to say is that we would love to

help you," Tina said, pumping the soaker again, "but your accusations are completely false. Go ahead. His locker is open. Check it if you don't believe me."

I held Tim tight with one hand as I rooted around his locker with the other.

The piece of wood wasn't there.

"OK, let go of my brother," Tina told me. "You have five seconds."

"No," I said. "Now we go to your locker."

"I don't think so," she said. "Now!"

Tim swung his right foot backward, trying to kick me in the shin. I backed away to avoid it, but in doing so, I lost some leverage on his arm. That was all he needed. He slipped out of my arm lock. Tina had a clear shot at me for half a second before a water balloon suddenly came out of nowhere and hit the locker next to her. She froze, staring at the water dripping down.

"Vinny Biggs sends his regards!" shouted a kid to my right. Three more balloons came flying at us. Tim dove and tackled his sister; a split second later, another water balloon passed through the space she had just been standing in. I shoved myself backward into Tim's locker and pulled the door closed, but with my finger still on the outside, keeping it from shutting completely and locking me inside. A balloon exploded against the door. Water dripped through the slats above, sprinkling down on me, but not enough to make an impact.

I could hear Vinny's hit kids running toward us. I tensed for a confrontation, waiting for the last possible moment before pushing the locker door open, hoping to time it perfectly and catch someone in the nose. If I timed it wrong, I'd be a sitting duck.

I waited . . . and waited . . . listening for a footstep outside the locker door. I heard the Thompsons run down the hall and two sets of footsteps running after them. I heard the sound of the exit door being slammed open in a hurry and the sound of footsteps running out and fading away. I heard the exit door squeak shut. Then I heard nothing.

I opened the locker door a crack and peeked out.

No one was there.

Even the spectators were gone.

I stepped out of the locker and looked around. I was alone.

I looked down at the puddles of water and the strips of rubber from exploded balloons that littered the hallway.

I tried not to think about how my job had put me in the wrong place at the wrong time again. That's all it would take—just one balloon, or one squirt of water. The only thing I had to defend myself with was luck. And I knew, somewhere in the school, there was a water balloon with my name on it, and that luck always ran out at the worst possible time.

"Balloons," came a voice from behind me. I wheeled around, arms cocked, ready to do some damage, but it was only Nicole Finnegan, a.k.a. the girl who used to be Nikki Fingers. Not so long ago, she was Vinny's most trusted lieutenant—and the Frank's most feared squirt-gun assassin. Then, a couple of weeks ago, her younger sister, Jenny, orchestrated a scheme to put Nikki in the Outs and take her place at Vinny's side. Now Nicole was just another broken kid, all traces of her fiery personality gone. Her red hair, which used to flow free and wild, hung limp and dull. You could say the same thing about the rest of her.

I lowered my arms. Her gaze was fixed on the spent balloons lying on the floor. "Balloons," she said again.

"Yeah," I said. I turned to leave. I wanted to get to Tina Thompson's locker before anyone else did. But it wasn't going to happen. Katie Kondo, chief hall monitor, was standing in my path.

"In a hurry, Stevens?" she asked.

"No, I'm just a speedy guy."

"Want to tell me what happened?" She pointed to the water and the balloon fragments on the floor.

I looked down as if I hadn't seen them before. "Wow! Looks like there's a litterbug loose," I replied. "All these popped balloons on the ground. And is that water? Why, someone could slip and fall!"

"Funny you're just noticing that now," she said.

"Nothing funny about it," I replied. "I've got a lot on my mind. Big project due."

"Oh yeah? What class is that?"

"Social studies."

"We're in that class together," she said. "I don't remember there being a project due."

"Well, you may be in trouble, then."

"Funny, I was just thinking the same thing about you."

"Balloons," the ghost of Nicole muttered, breaking the tension.

I looked at her. For a second, I thought Katie was going to haul Nicole into detention for even daring to speak. But Katie didn't react. If anything, her expression softened for a moment. "Thanks," she said. "I can see that. How did they get here?"

"Why don't you find the people who dropped them and ask?" I said.

Her expression hardened. "I heard you were on the scene when Melissa got put in the Outs just now, Stevens. Why am I not surprised?"

"Because nothing surprises you anymore. You've forgotten how to believe in magic!" I said. "Funny . . . I don't remember seeing you there. Little slow getting around these days?"

Katie leaned toward me. "You helped my sister, Matt . . . and I haven't forgotten that," she growled, as if she'd like nothing better than to forget it. "But you just used up your last free pass. Got it?"

"Not really," I said. "I had free passes?!? And now they're gone?!? How many did I start with? And when did I use the others? Can I trade them in for cash and prizes?"

Katie's lips started twitching, as if they couldn't wait to get a taste of my blood. She opened her mouth to say something, but Nicole spoke first. "Balloons," she said, pointing to the floor this time. She looked up at us, wide-eyed.

Katie looked over at her; I could feel the momentum

of her anger grinding to a halt. She took a deep breath, then looked back at me. "Get out of here, Stevens."

"Will do, Chief," I said as I walked down the hall. "Glad to see those anger-management classes are paying off."

I walked away as quickly as I could without running. The last thing I heard before I was out of earshot was Nicole saying "Balloons" again, and Katie quietly agreeing with her.

6

$\mathcal{I}$ had staked out Tina Thompson on a past case, so I knew her locker was one of a handful placed in a small alcove under a staircase, almost as if the school had put them in as an afterthought. I couldn't remember which locker was hers, but it turned out that I didn't need to. Of the eight lockers, one had been pried open. The metal all around the edge of the door had been bent, as if someone with a crowbar couldn't find a weak point and had decided to sculpt the door into an entirely new shape. Whatever their plan, it seemed to have worked.

I looked up the stairwell to see if anyone was coming. Then I tried to look inside the locker without touching the door or opening it any farther, but the gap wasn't wide enough to see anything. After one more stairway check, I used my foot to open the door all the way, so I wouldn't leave any fingerprints.

There, sitting on the top shelf, as if waiting patiently for me, was the missing piece of wood.

I picked it up. It was small—as small and thin as a piece of white bread. It had an intricately carved pattern on one side. There was a sticky note attached to it. It was a message, in handwriting I didn't recognize. It said, "Go for the skirt." I was pretty sure it wasn't a fashion tip. Someone had told the Thompsons about Melissa, which meant that my incompetence was only partly responsible for her getting popped. It made me feel a little better, but not much.

I shoved the note in my front pocket, then put the piece of wood in my back pocket. There was a sandwich bag full of Pixy Stix on the floor of the locker. I grabbed it and put it in my other back pocket. Then I pulled my shirt low to cover everything. I hoped that no one decided to do a close examination of my tush.

I closed the locker door and walked away.

The hallways were deserted. I walked to the main entrance of the school. I could still hear the basketball sounds, though I was far from the gym. The cheering. The game sounds. As if the past hour hadn't happened. As if a cheerleader's life hadn't just skidded off the road. I pushed open the doors and walked out.

It was starting to get dark now that daylight saving time had ended. The air was cold, but it was still comfortable enough for walking. I thought about going to Sal's for a root beer or six but then thought better of it. It was a game day, so people would already be there, drinking. If we won, they'd keep drinking to celebrate; if we lost, they'd keep drinking to drown their sorrows. I didn't really feel like being around people. Oh, and I just happened to have a thing in my back pocket that some of the shadiest, most powerful kids in school were fighting over. Oh, and a full bag of designer Pixy Stix. I decided it might be best if I just went home.

When I got there, my mom was just leaving the house to go to her second job: a waitressing gig at Santini's, an upscale restaurant downtown. Ever since my dad disappeared over six years ago, she's had to carry two jobs just to almost-but-not-quite make ends meet. Usually, we got along great—our relationship was a nice mixture of respect and protectiveness. But lately things had been a little strained.

"No need to lock it," I said.

"Oh! Hey!" my mom replied, turning around. Her purse squirted out from under her arm. She was able to snatch it in midair before it hit the ground, but her lip balm flew out and rolled to a stop at my feet.

"Was that an overelaborate way of letting me know that my lips are chapped?" I asked as I picked it up. "Because you could have just told me."

"I didn't want to hurt your feelings," she replied. "I know how sensitive you are about your lips."

"I think they're my third best feature, right behind my intellect and sharp wit . . ."

"Of course. Although I should ask your girlfriend for a more accurate grading."

I blushed. I wasn't sure I was comfortable discussing my "girlfriend" with my mom.

"Right," she said to fill in the awkward silence where my response was supposed to fit. She walked past me toward the car.

I turned and smiled at her. "Say hi to Mr. Carling for me." Kevin and Liz's dad, Albert Carling, managed Santini's. My mom did NOT get along with him.

"That's enough, chappy!"

"Hey! I'm sensitive!" I said in mock outrage. I picked up the lip balm, took the cap off, and slathered it sloppily all over my face. I put the cap back on, then offered it back to my mom.

"Ugh," she said. "Feel free to keep that." She checked her watch. "All right, I have to go. Come here and give your mom a kiss."

I walked over with my lips puckered. They glistened, thick with lip balm. My mom grabbed both sides of my head. She gripped tight, and planted a big kiss on my forehead.

"I love ya," she said, "but greasy lips are where I draw the line." I smiled. "I'll be home at two," she continued. "Don't—"

"—wait up. Yeah, I know. See you at two."

Just then the phone in the basement started ringing.

"Ugh. That damn thing's been ringing off the hook since I got home," she said. "I wish the landlord would just take it out."

"Yeah," I said, even though I didn't mean it. That phone was supposed to be a private line for the landlord, but I was pretty sure I used it more than he did.

"All right. Spaghetti's in the fridge."

"Okay. Love ya."

"Back atcha." She smiled halfheartedly at me, as if she hated the fact that these two minutes were our catch-up time for the day. But there was nothing either of us could do about it.

I walked inside, closed the door, and headed straight for the basement.

The phone had stopped ringing by the time I picked it up. There was only a dial tone, so I hung up and sat down at my desk.

My mom and I lived in the first-floor apartment, and we had the only indoor access to the basement. The only other person that came down here was the guy who owned the building, some guy called "Big A." At least, I thought Big A owned it. Every once in a while, I'd get a call from some guy looking for "Big A." Whenever I tried to take a message, though, he'd hang up.

Other than Big A (who I never saw), no one else came down here, not even my mom. It was a storage space, and quite frankly, when you don't have much, you don't really need extra storage. There were a bunch of boxes of holiday decorations and old toys of mine that my mom didn't have the heart to throw out, but still more than enough space for me to set up shop.

I was able to furnish my office with rich people's "junk." Rich people apparently have a different definition of junk than I do. To me, junk is something that doesn't work anymore; to them, junk is something that doesn't match the new pillows they just bought.

I had an old wood desk and matching chair, a beat-up but comfortable sofa with a faded floral slipcover, a couple of lamps, and an old-fashioned radio that had needed quite a bit of elbow grease to get working again. It was my own office: a little dark, a little musty, and totally private—crucial for a business like mine.

I pulled the piece of wood out of my back pocket and put it on the desk. Before I studied it, I did what I always do when I come down to my office. I opened the center drawer on my desk and pulled out the sheet of paper they'd found in my dad's car five days after he went missing. The car was in a parking garage, four states away; this paper was in the glove compartment. On the sheet of paper, neatly typed in the left corner, was: TMS136P15. I had been turning it over in my head for years and still had no idea what it meant.

The phone rang. I picked it up. "Yeah?"

"Matt?"

"As far as you know."

"It's Kevin. Where've you been? I've been trying to call you."

"Yeah, so I heard. You should really switch to decaf."

"What the hell happened today?" he yelled.

"Don't pretend you don't already know."

"Listen, man, Vinny thinks you weren't being completely honest with him. He seems to think that you knew Melissa had the piece of wood he was looking for."

"And if I did?"

Kevin sighed heavily.

"You should hold the phone away from your mouth before you do that," I said. "I can practically feel your spit in my ear."

"Do you have the piece of wood?"

"I don't want to talk about it."

"That means yes," he said. "Or no."

"Well, as long as you've got it narrowed down to those two choices . . ."

"Listen, Matt, I know we haven't been the best of friends lately, but— I mean, you really saved my butt a couple of weeks ago. Come on, let me help you."

"Nothing to help with, Kev. Really."

There was a pause.

"All right," he said. "Listen, Matt . . . I'm serious . . . don't stonewall yourself right into the Outs, okay? Ask for help if you need it."

"All right," I said. And I meant it.

"See you in school tomorrow," he said.

"Now how am I supposed to sleep tonight, with all this anticipation!"

He laughed. "Shut up."

"I'll dream of you," I whispered.

"Ugh," he said, and hung up.

I put the receiver back in the cradle. The phone rang again immediately. I picked it up.

"Yeah?"

"Matt?"

"Hold on, let me check . . . Yeah, it's me."

"It's Mac." Jimmy MacGregor was the editor of the school paper and one of the few honest kids at the Frank. "Where ya been? I been trying to reach ya."

"Yeah, so I heard. You should really switch to decaf."

"Nah. I'd miss the jitters too much. Listen, can you meet me at Sal's?"

"When?"

"In three weeks," he said. "Now! Why do you think I've been calling?"

"Because you missed me and my sparkling brown eyes? Hey, don't you have a newspaper to put out or something?"

"I don't tell you your job, do I?"

"The way I've been doing it lately, maybe you should. Listen, I've already had a busy day," I said. "Can this wait until I recover? Say, in four to six months?"

"Stop being such a sissy and meet me at Sal's in five minutes. You'll thank me."

"Can I just thank you now and not go?" I asked, but he had already hung up. I had to hand it to him; he had given me just enough info to make me curious but not enough to know what he was talking about. It looked like I was going to Sal's after all.

I picked the wooden block up off of my desk and looked around the basement for a place to hide it.

I had an old metal filing cabinet that I kept my case files in. There was no lock on it, but the bottom drawer stuck. I pushed on the side of the cabinet and jiggled the drawer in the special way it took to get it open. Then I put the block of wood, and the bag of designer Pixy Stix, underneath a stack of old school papers. It was the best I could do at the moment.

I headed outside, locked the door, checked it twice, then pedaled off to Sal's.

As I was riding to Sal's, I went over the events of the day. I was trying to wrap my head around the particulars of the case, but like a board game bought at a tag sale, there were a bunch of pieces missing. Melissa Scott (cheerleader, member of the popular elite) hires me to watch her boyfriend, Will Atkins (captain of the basketball team, most elite member of the popular elite), because she thinks he's acting strange. Also, he gives her a block of wood to hold but tells her it's no big deal. It may not be a big deal to him, but it turns out that it's a big deal to Vinny Biggs and the Thompsons, which pretty much guarantees there's something fishy about it. Melissa gets put in the Outs by the Thompsons, who take the block of wood. Then someone opens Tina Thompson's locker like a tin can but leaves the wood inside. Why? What was so special about this particular "decorative piece of wood"? And who gave it to Will to hold in the first place?

It was a week before Halloween, so some of the lawns looked like sets for low-budget horror movies. The air had a bite to it that wasn't there a couple of weeks ago, and I knew that pretty soon it'd be too cold to ride my bike. The wind would freeze my face off.

Sal Becker was a kid in my class who wanted to make a place where kids could get a sandwich and a soda without having to deal with the "grown-up shuffle" that kids had to face in most places. So Sal and his dad spent the summer fixing up the big old toolshed that was sitting to the side of their house. They put in a bar and some tables, made the place look nice without looking too showy. Various tag-sale lamps were scattered around, giving the place a warm, inviting glow. Sal had a little toaster oven behind the bar and could whip up a toasted cheese sandwich, or a peanut butter and jelly (strawberry or grape). Those were the only two things on the menu. He also served root beer and cream soda—the good kind, in glass bottles. His parents let him run the place himself. They only had two rules: no fighting and no fighting.

I walked in and grabbed a cream soda at the bar. Jimmy was sitting at a table in the back with Cynthia Shea. She was wearing sweats and a baseball cap pulled low over her eyes, trying her best to look inconspicuous. It was like trying to hide a Porsche by putting a napkin over it. When Jimmy saw me, he stood up and waved.

"Mac," I said, trying to keep my voice from cracking.

"Matt. This is Cynthia—"

"Shea," I said finishing his sentence. "Head cheer-leader."

"We met earlier today," she said.

"Twice," I countered. "And so far, we're oh-for-two. So what's the plan for the third time? You going to punch me out or just have me arrested?"

"I want to hire you," she said.

"I don't hire myself out for abuse. Plus, I'm sure you can find someone who'll let you yell at them for free, just for your attention."

"I'm sorry about earlier. Jimmy here vouches for you. That's good enough for me."

"Cynthia's family and mine go way back," Mac added. I looked at him. He was more hyped up than usual, which I didn't think was possible.

"That's great. Congratulations," I said. "If you're trying to hire me to find out who pulled the trigger on Melissa, you're too late."

"Who?" Cynthia asked.

I didn't answer.

She looked at Jimmy, who just shrugged. I couldn't tell if he didn't know or was just bluffing.

"Who?" she repeated.

"Why do you want to know?" I asked. "So you can find them? Get a little revenge?"

"No," she said.

"Yeah, next time try saying it without gritting your teeth," I said. "You might be more convincing."

"Did it have something to do with these?" She threw a handful of the Thompsons' special Pixy Stix on the table.

Jimmy Mac's eyes opened wide, as if she had just handed him a lit stick of dynamite. "Where'd you get those?" he whispered.

"Did it?" she asked me without even looking at Jimmy.

I didn't answer. Jimmy tried to pick the Pixy Stix up off the table, but Cynthia put her hand on top of his.

Once he stopped trying, she took her hand away. He left his hand on the table, obviously hoping she'd do it again.

"Melissa was a client of yours, wasn't she?" she asked.

"I know you're used to getting your way," I said, "so this is going to be a major disappointment, but that is none of your business."

"Hey, come on, Matt," Jimmy Mac said. "I know her. I'm vouching for her."

"Don't take this the wrong way, Jimmy, but judging by what I've seen so far, you'd vouch for her about anything . . . even if she said she was the queen of England and had traveled here from Mars."

"Is there a right way to take that, jerk?" he asked.

"To hell with you, Mac." I stood up. My chair made a loud raspberry as it skidded on the floor. "I don't appreciate you springing this surprise two-against-one consultation about what my next job should be."

"Shut up!" Cynthia yelled. If the kids who were in Sal's hadn't been staring at her already, they were now. "Cut all this macho posturing! Both of you."

I glared at her, but she glared back at me. I learned a long time ago that there was no way to win a staring contest—or a glaring contest—with a pretty girl. I sat down and looked away.

Cynthia leaned over and whispered in Mac's ear. He had a dreamy look on his face, like he had waited his entire life for this scenario. But Cynthia must've whispered something different in Mac's dream scenario than in the one playing out in real life, because by the time she finished, his expression had changed to a bucket of ice-cold realization.

"I have to go," Jimmy said in a stiff voice. "Paper's due out tomorrow." He got up to leave, slowly, as if he were hoping for Cynthia to reconsider and stop him. She didn't. After a few seconds, he accepted his fate and walked toward the door. I grunted at him as he passed; he grunted back.

Cynthia waited until he was gone before she spoke again. "You guys couldn't have apologized to each other?"

"What do you think that grunt was? Jeez, for guys, that's practically falling into each other's arms."

She was giving me a long hard look. I could see it out of the corner of my eye. There was no way I was going to look at her directly. She was too pretty, and I needed to remain professional.

"Why are you angry with me?" she asked. It was an odd question, and the last thing I expected.

"What makes you think I'm angry with you? I don't even know you."

"I was just thinking the same thing. And yet here you are, acting like I'm your mortal enemy."

"Let's just say I have a hard time talking to girls who expect the world to collapse at their feet when they bat their eyelashes."

"I haven't batted them once," she said.

"No, but I did see you purse your lips a couple of times."

"Are you watching my lips?" she asked. A small smile started to creep across her mouth.

"Uhhh . . ." was all I could muster. The supersmooth Matt Stevens strikes again.

"Forget it. I withdraw the question," she said. "So can I hire you, or what?"

"Or what, for the moment," I said. I pointed to the Pixy Stix still on the table. "Where'd you get these?"

"Some of the girls on the squad. They use them before a game sometimes."

"You allow that?"

"No, but they do it anyway," she said, obviously not happy about it. "Well, they *did*. As of today, they can suck down as many Stix as they want . . . they just won't be cheerleaders anymore."

"What makes you think these have something to do with Melissa getting popped?"

"Do you know who makes them? The Thompsons," she said. "They look like they'd pop their own grandmother for a couple of nickels."

"Or a piece of wood."

"What?"

"Nothing."

"If the Thompsons were the ones who put Melissa in the Outs—" she started.

"You're afraid they're going to go after the rest of the squad, now that they're no longer buying."

She nodded.

"And you're here to protect 'your girls'?" I asked.

"This," she said, pointing to the cheerleading patch on the jacket hanging off the back of her chair, "is a sisterhood. We look out for each other."

"Oh yeah? Like you looked out for Gretchen Jacobson? She was on the squad last year, wasn't she? Yet when Vinny and his crew put her in the Outs, your 'sisters' knocked her off the squad, then took turns kicking her around. That 'sisterhood' garbage may work on the parents and new recruits, but it doesn't fly with someone who's been around."

"Yeah . . . but I'm in charge now," she said. "If I say we take care of our own, then we take care of our own."

I shrugged.

"You don't believe me?" she asked.

"Does it matter to you what I believe?"

"Not yet, but it might."

I didn't believe her on that point, either, and I gave her a look that told her so. "Why do you do it?" I asked.

"What?"

"Cheerlead. It's a status grab. Nothing more. But you don't seem like that type of girl. So what gives?" I asked.

"What 'type of girl'? You mean stupid and shallow?"

"You said it, I didn't."

"But you were thinking it."

I didn't deny it.

She sighed. "Look, I'm not going to lie. Status wasn't the main reason I joined the squad, but it was definitely in my top five."

"You keep a list?"

She shot me a sarcastic smile, then continued. "But there is also this feeling of performing . . . of dancing . . . of getting people excited and cheering and pumped. The adrenaline rush is addictive. Plus, I get to be part of something that's bigger than me . . . a sisterhood with traditions and—"

"Come on," I said, cutting her off. "Some of those girls would be hard to take if you were related to them and you had no choice. You're either in denial, or you have a high tolerance for being around really annoying girls."

"Again, why are you angry with me? Is it because I don't fit in to one of your neat little boxes?" She leaned in close. "Is it because I scare you?"

"Look, I know this whole 'flirty' act is just to get me to do what you want, but I'm not buying it. You're probably going to leave here and call your basketball-player boyfriend."

"I don't have a boyfriend . . . yet." She stared into my eyes. I tried to look away but found that I couldn't.

"Here," she said, and slid a five-dollar bill across the table. "I believe that's your usual deposit."

"I didn't say yes."

She brought her face inches from mine. "Do these look like the eyes of someone who just gives up?" she asked.

I swallowed hard, then slowly shook my head no. Her face lingered in front of mine for a moment longer, as if to say, "If you take my case, you'll be able to look at this face more often." It was a convincing argument.

"So what would you be hiring me to do?" I asked.

"You know who did this to Melissa. Do whatever it takes to keep it from happening to anyone else on the squad."

"People who say 'Do whatever it takes' usually have no idea what that actually means."

"That's why I'm hiring you," she said. "I have a feeling you do."

She stood up. I stood up with her. She held out her hand. I shook it. She held on. "I'll check in with you tomorrow," she said. I was going to say that I still hadn't taken the case, but there was no use. We both knew I had, just not verbally. Our eyes locked. We both blushed. She let my hand go, then turned, swept her jacket off the back of the chair, and walked out the door. I slumped back down into my chair, exhausted.

Sal came over with another cream soda. "On the house," he said, and winked. I didn't argue.

• • •

Twenty minutes later, I was riding my bike home, trying to think of something other than Cynthia Shea holding my hand, saying that she'd see me tomorrow. I wasn't doing so hot. The only thing I could come up with was wondering how "Sucker-for-a-Cheerleader Detective Agency" would look on a business card.

It was around eight when I got home. My mom was still a good six hours from the end of her shift at the restaurant, so I went down to my office to examine the block of wood. Before I took it out it, I checked the dark corners of the basement for anyone who might be hidden there. I even opened the door to the outside and checked the bushes, then went back inside and locked the door behind me. I opened the drawer to the filing cabinet. I half expected it not to be there, but it was. Right where I had left it.

I went back to my desk and sat down. Apparently, I had forgotten to put the sheet of paper with my father's clue back in my desk drawer because it lay on the desk. I turned the block of wood over in my hands, noticing the grain and wondering what was so important about this thing that kids would splash each other to get their hands on it. I gave it a little shake. Something rattled. I felt like an idiot for not thinking of that sooner.

It wasn't a block of wood; it was a box.

I looked at each side, trying to find an obvious seam, but there wasn't one. It was a trick box, designed to prevent people from taking whatever was inside. I shook it. It rattled again, but this time I noticed that it only rattled on one end. I tapped that end, but nothing happened. I tapped the bottom. Nothing happened. I tapped the other end. Something inside clicked, and a small piece of wood slid out. The grain of the wood had hidden the seam.

I looked inside, expecting to see something small but solid, like a coin or a plastic trinket . . . something to explain the rattle. I was wrong. The rattle was caused by the magnet that served as the latch for the hidden door. Inside there was only a small slip of paper. I turned the box upside down, and the piece of paper fluttered onto my desktop, like a moth that had croaked mid-flight. There was something written on the paper, something I recognized, but at first, my mind wouldn't accept it as real. I rubbed my eyes and looked again. It was real.

There were now two pieces of paper on my desk: one

from my desk drawer, which I had never shown anyone before, and one from the wooden box I got in school that day. The pieces of paper were different in every way, except one . . . they both had TMS136P15 written on them.

That's not possible," I said out loud, as if hearing it would make me believe it more. I had never shown that sheet of paper to another person. No one. It wasn't possible. And yet, there it was.

My mind was racing, running through every possibility as to how and why a clue to my father's disappearance had ended up in a wood box that caused my most recent client to gt banished to the Outs. The first thing I did was check my desk drawer, the one where I kept the original clue. I didn't keep it locked, so there wouldn't be any signs of forced entry. But I've had people go through my stuff before—mostly in my locker at school—and no matter how much they'd try to hide it, there was always a feeling like something was off . . . like my mind was carrying around a subconscious picture of the inside of my locker, and someone's digging, regardless of how careful they were, always screwed that picture up. I wasn't getting that feeling about my drawer.

I got up and checked the lock on the outside door. It was intact. No one had tampered with it. I could have left it unlocked. Locking a door is something you do thousands of times, so that you never really notice if you remember to do it. But you do remember if you come home to an unlocked door, and I hadn't had any moments like that in the recent past.

Could someone have gotten this information from an outside source? Who? And from where?

I kept coming back to one name, the one kid who ended up being involved in every dirty deal that went down at the Frank . . . the one kid who always seemed to be five to ten steps ahead of everyone else. I grabbed my address book, picked up the phone, and punched in the numbers. He picked up on the third ring.

"Biggio residence, Vincent speaking."

"I found it."

He paused. I heard him exhale slowly. "Did you, now?" he asked.

"I did, but there's a problem."

"Is there, now?"

"Yeah," I said, "and it's even worse than you putting 'now' at the end of all of your questions. Did you know it isn't just a piece of wood? It's a box."

"Matthew, I do not wish to discuss this over the ph—"

"What am I saying? Of course you knew it was a box. Didn't think to tell me, though, did you?"

"You didn't need to know."

"Really. Because from where I'm sitting, the stakes for a piece of wood are vastly different than the stakes for a box . . . especially when what we're *really* talking about is what's inside that box. And that's what this is all about, isn't it? What's inside the box." I picked up the piece of paper that had fallen out. "The Thompsons knew it was a box . . . probably even knew what was inside it, which is why you sent your thugs after them."

"And now you have it."

"I do."

"And you want something."

"Yeah, you could say that."

Vinny sighed. "Well, this is surprising. I must say, Matthew, I never expected this from you."

"Never expected what?"

"Oh, come now. We both know what this is about. It's actually a momentous occasion. Finally, something valuable enough to make Saint Matthew Stevens step down off his high horse." He laughed. "For once, I wish this line wasn't secure, so someone else could bear witness to this."

"What the hell are you talking about?" I asked.

"I understand. You don't want to say the word. It's too dirty. Fine. I'll say it for you. Blackmail."

"Wha— Blackmail?"

"Yes, Matthew. Blackmail. Maybe you're calling it something different in your head," he said, "hoping that a different label will allow you to hold on to the pristine image you have of yourself. But blackmail under any other name is still blackmail."

"I . . . ," I started, but I had no idea how to continue. I picked up the piece of paper I had found in the box, hoping that it would give me some clue as to what

Vinny was talking about, but it only brought up more questions.

"Relax, Matthew. As I mentioned before, this is a secure line. So, since you've never done this before, let me tell you how it works. Now is the time when you tell me what you want. Then I decide whether to give it to you or just destroy you and take my chances. So tell me, Matthew . . . what is it that you want?"

"I want to know what this piece of paper has to do with *you* and why you would possibly think that I would use it to blackmail you," I said.

"Piece of paper . . . ," he said, trying to keep the confusion out of his voice and mostly succeeding.

"You thought it was something different," I said.

He paused before answering. "Perhaps."

"What did you think I'd found?"

"I'd rather not say," he said. "What did you actually find?"

"I'd rather not say."

"Interesting," he purred. "Matt Stevens has some secrets of his own." His voice was hopeful and greedy. "So now what?"

"So now nothing," I said. "You hired me to find this piece of wood. I found it."

"That's not the deal anymore."

"What, you think you can just renegotiate whenever it suits you?"

"Yes. I do. Forty dollars says I can."

"You can have that back," I said. "If it'll make you feel better, I can stuff it inside the box before I give it to you."

"I don't want my money back. I want to retain your services."

"No."

"Matthew, as far as our relationship is concerned, the word 'no' has been removed from your vocabulary."

"In that case, ask me if I think you're a jerk."

He chuckled. "Touché."

"I'm always surprised when you resort to bullying to get your way, Vinny . . . considering what you used to go through."

"I'm always surprised by your surprise, Matthew . . . considering what I used to go through," he said. "The thing is, I haven't changed. I'm still the same kid I was when I was getting knocked around. The only difference is, I now have the means to get what I want."

"I wouldn't say that's the only difference."

"Yes, well, only because you didn't know me very well back then."

"I knew you well enough to think you were worth protecting from bullies," I said.

Vinny was quiet.

"Good night, Matthew," he said, finally. "I'm going to need you tomorrow. I'll let you know when you're available."

Before I could respond, he hung up.

It was two in the morning when I heard the door to our apartment open. I was lying in bed, staring up at the ceiling, trying to find one spot on my pillow that was still cool. I heard my mom tiptoe down the hallway, then slowly open my bedroom door. I thought about pretending to be asleep, but I was too wired to fake it.

"Hey," she said. "You're awake." She stood in the doorway but didn't come inside. Her shape was silhouetted by the light of the hallway, and I couldn't see her face.

"Don't sound so surprised," I said. "Aren't I always?"

"Yeah, but usually you're just barely hanging in there. Tonight, you're *wide* awake. Is everything okay?"

What answer could I give? *Not really . . . see, this girl at school hired me for a job, but then she had her life ruined because of this decorative little box. Actually, it wasn't because of the box; it was because of what was* inside *the box. What*

was inside the box? Well, apparently not what was supposed
to be in there. What was supposed *to be in the box was
something that someone could use to blackmail Vinny Biggs,
if they were into that sort of thing. (Vinny Biggs is the head of
a whole criminal organization at school and he uses his power
to destroy kids' lives by putting them in the Outs . . . but
that's a discussion for another time.) What was* actually *in
the box was a piece of paper with the same letter and number
sequence that they found in Dad's car when he disappeared.
Other than that, I'm fine.*

Instead, I just said, "Yup."

"I never trust one-word answers," she said, "especially
when they come after three-minute pauses."

I shrugged. "Not sure what to tell you."

"Are you sure that you're not sure?"

"No," I said. "In fact, I'm sure that I'm not sure that
I'm sure."

"Sure you are," she said.

I smiled. I think she smiled, too, but because of the
shadows, I couldn't tell.

"You want to talk about it?" she asked.

"I do, but I don't. And I can't . . ."

"So you won't," she said. "Yeah . . . I get it." There was
something in her voice that made me sit up. I reached for

the lamp on my bedside table. When I turned on the light, I saw that her eyes were bloodshot and puffy. Her nose was red. She'd been crying.

"What happened?" I asked.

"You first," she said.

"This . . . no . . . We talked about this," I said. "We agreed to keep our own secrets. But if one of us got in over our heads, we'd ask the other for help."

"And you think I'm in over my head?" she asked. "How did you come to that conclusion?"

"You're kidding, right? You're—" I stopped. "You're crying," I said, making an effort not to start crying myself.

"And you're lying in your bed, wide awake at two in the morning," she said. "So, what conclusion should I come to?"

I didn't say anything.

I understood her position, but that didn't keep me from feeling frustrated. I wanted to be there for her, to help her . . . and I imagined she was feeling the same thing about me.

She walked into my room and sat down on the edge of my bed.

"We've kind of painted ourselves into a corner," I said.

My mom nodded. "Any ideas on what to do next?"

"No. Hey, aren't you an adult? Don't you have any age-related wisdom you can apply to this situation?"

"Age-related wisdom?!?" she said, laughing. "That's the worst euphemism for 'old' I've ever heard." She reached over and mussed up my hair, then pushed my head back so that it fell into the pillow. "Think of that as a little nudge toward dreamland," she said.

"More like a shove toward Concussion City."

She stood up and walked out the door, then stopped and turned. "Are you sure you can handle what's going on?" she asked.

"No. Are you?"

"No. When do you think you'll know for sure?"

"Probably when it's too late to ask for help," I said.

"Yeah. Me too."

"Well, at least now I know who I inherited *that* from," I said.

"Good night, Matt. Try to get some sleep."

"Back atcha."

I used to think I trusted my mom, that I could tell her anything . . . which was ridiculous, considering that

I couldn't tell her anything about what really happened at the Frank. So, which was better: the lie that was comfortable or the truth that made me wish we were still living the lie?

Tuesday morning came. There was no way to stop it. The best I could do was delay it a bit. After several trips to the snooze bar, I realized that I wasn't going to feel rested by getting sleep in ten-minute increments. I rolled out of bed, turned off the alarm, and stumbled into the day. Getting through school on two hours of sleep wasn't ideal, but I had done it enough times to know it was possible.

In the kitchen, there was a ten-dollar bill and a note from my mom. "Don't spend this all on coffee," it said.

"Love ya." I smiled. I picked up the ten dollars and walked down the hall toward her room. She had an ugly ceramic pineapple on top of her dresser where she kept her emergency fund. I picked up the lid and stuffed the ten inside. I still had almost fifty bucks from three different clients; no need to take my mom's money. I stumbled back to the kitchen to start my morning routine.

As I drank some juice and poured myself some cereal, my thoughts shifted to the piece of paper inside the box. Who put it there and why? And how did they know about TMS136P15? Had they somehow been involved in my dad's disappearance? Was putting that code in the box an attempt to hurt or distract me, or was someone trying to make contact with me? Or did it have nothing to do with me? Was TMS136P15 part of something bigger, and my dad's disappearance was only a small part of it?

My head started hurting; it didn't feel big enough to hold the number of possibilities that I was going to have to sift through in order to get some answers. I decided that the best way to move forward with this case was to start at the beginning, with Will Atkins. He was the one who had given Melissa the box to hold in the first place, and he had told her not to tell anyone she had it because it might be valuable. It was valuable, all right. It was time to find out if Will knew why.

I grabbed the school newspaper as I walked into the building and saw that Will had won the game almost single-handedly, scoring forty-two of Franklin's sixty-one points, including the game winner at the buzzer. He even used his post-game remarks to make a statement about some "activities in this school that need to stop. We're on the same team; we should act like it." My feelings for Will were definitely conflicted.

I checked in with a contact in the principal's office. The Thompsons were listed as absent. That should've made me feel a little less anxious, but there were a lot of rocks to hide under at the Frank, and I was pretty sure that the Thompsons had at some time or other crawled under most of them.

When I wasn't looking over my shoulder, I watched Will. He went through his usual morning routine of soaking up the adoration of our classmates. No one seemed to offer any condolences for what had happened to his girlfriend, although a couple of girls did "accidentally" trip and stumble right into him.

Apart from all the attention, he did the same things I had seen him do the previous day: He hummed his song, tapped his locker, smiled and chatted with his stream of fans . . . but there was definitely something different about him. He was twitchy in a way that seemed different from his game-day jitters.

Then, right after third period, he spotted me. He had locked his locker, tapped on the door four times, and started to walk to class when our eyes met. He pretended like he didn't see me. When he reached the doors to the gym, he went inside. Not wanting to be obvious, or to get jumped, I continued down the hall. I kept walking until I came to another set of doors, the ones leading to the other side of the gym. I opened those doors as quietly as possible and slipped inside.

Will was at the free throw line at the far end. He dribbled in place a couple of times, took a deep breath, bent his knees slowly, then came back up smoothly, with perfect form, his arm going from bent to straight, his wrist going from bent back to bent forward: the perfect "gooseneck" necessary to give the ball backspin. The ball swished through the net, then bounced and rolled back to him, like a well-trained dog returning to its master. He picked it up and held it.

"Can I help you with something?" he asked, without even turning toward me.

I looked around the gym, to see if there was anyone else he could be talking to. There wasn't.

"Come on, man," he said. "I spend the majority of my time in this gym. I'm in here more than I'm in my own home. I know every click of every door, every creak of every floorboard. No matter how quiet you think you are, I can hear you." He repeated the same perfect free throw motion as before, with the same exact result. He picked up the ball again and turned to face me.

"Matt Stevens," I said, and started walking toward him.

"I've heard of you," he said. "Kids hire you to do stuff for them, right?"

"That's one way to put it."

"So, did someone hire you to watch me? Is that why you're here?" he asked.

I stopped walking. We were six or seven feet apart. He lifted the ball slowly, as if he was getting ready to throw a chest pass. He seemed friendly, but I got the feeling that if I made a sudden movement, that's exactly what he'd do.

"Melissa hired me to watch you," I said. He grimaced at the mention of her name. "She was worried about you."

He sighed. "Poor Melissa. I wish someone had been more worried about her."

"I was. It didn't help. Maybe if you hadn't given her that box to hold."

Just mentioning the box had the effect of a ten-thousand-volt current going through his body. His eyes shot open wide; his head jerked back. He raised the ball in his right hand like a baseball; his feet shifted like a shortstop preparing to throw a runner out at first. "You have five seconds to tell me the truth or I break your nose."

I almost said *Calm down*, which was something you never want to say in such a situation. Someone that worked up was liable to smack you for even suggesting he calm down. Instead, I said, "You gave your girlfriend, Melissa Scott, a box to hold, right?"

"It wasn't a box," he replied. "It was just a piece of wood. Like a decoration or a knickknack . . ."

"Is that what your friend told you when he gave it to you?"

"Yeah, he—" Will stopped. "I don't have to tell you anything." The ball was still in his hand.

"You're right. You don't. But at this moment, I may be the most important person in your life," I said. "And you do not want to break the nose of the most important person in your life."

"Explain. Two seconds."

"I'm not the only person who knows it's a box. Vinny Biggs and the Thompsons know it, too. Even worse, they know what's inside. And they want it . . . and they're willing to put anyone and everyone in the Outs until they get their hands on it. And when I say 'anyone and everyone,' that includes the captain of the basketball team."

He stood there thinking about it, still ready to chuck the ball at my face if the conversation called for it. He could do some damage, too. "I'm supposed to take the word of some shady kid who's stalking me?"

"Whoa, whoa, whoa," I said. "I'm more shifty than shady. You can ask anyone. As for the stalking part, as I said, Melissa hired me to do it."

"How do I know you weren't the one who put Melissa—"

The door behind him opened. He turned with the basketball still cocked, as if the play was now at second base instead of first. Vinny's two guards, the ones who "retrieved" me yesterday at lunch, walked in. Vinny was behind them, flanked by a couple more of his "employees."

Robbie "Mouse" Mariano was one of them. A short, skinny kid with glasses, Robbie was Vinnie's numbers guy. He went to the high school three times a week to take math classes because he had completed the requirements for middle school when he was in the third grade.

The other kid with Vinny was Jenny Finnegan.

A few feet into the gym, both guards stopped. Vinny, Robbie, and Jenny walked between them. A few feet more, Robbie and Jenny stopped. Vinny kept coming until there was only a foot or so of empty space between him and Will.

"Nice choreography," I said. "Looks like you guys have been practicing."

Vinny ignored me. Jenny gave me a sneer, large enough that she could get her point across but small enough that Vinny couldn't see it. Will's arm was still in the same throwing position, but it had drooped a little.

"William," Vinny said, "I would like to talk to Matthew."

Will turned and gave me a triumphant smile, as if all of his suspicions about me were right, and this just proved it. I shrugged. Now wasn't the time to try to change his mind.

"Why don't you go practice your free throws at the other end of the court," Vinny added. It wasn't a question.

Will paused, as if he wasn't used to taking orders from someone who didn't have a whistle around his neck. I wondered for a moment if he was going to give Vinny a speech about how this was his court, but then the ball fell out of his hand and bounced on the floor. He turned that bounce into a lazy dribble and started walking to the other end of the court.

Vinny came over to me. The rest of his entourage stayed put. "Matthew, I told you that you would be available to me at some point today. We have arrived at some point."

"I see you brought some trusted employees with you," I said. "Oh, and Jenny. Hey, Jenny! How's your sister, Nicole? She forgive you for what you did to her yet?"

She took a step toward me; her sneer got a little bigger. "If she was as good as everybody thought she was, she wouldn't be in the Outs, now, would she?" Jenny said in a sweet, mocking voice. "Hope you're ready to join her, Matty."

"Jennifer," Vinny said without turning around.

Jenny looked at him, considered her options, then

backed up to her original position. She shot me a dirty look, but there was no force behind it.

I smiled. "You yank a good leash, Vinny. 'Sit, Jenny. Stay.' "

Jenny's sneer turned into a snarl.

"Matthew," Vinny said. "Don't overstep your bounds."

I stopped. Now wasn't the time to push my luck. "All right. So what are you going to start with this time?" I asked. "Money or force? Bribe or threat? Choices, choices, choices . . ."

"Matthew, you seem to be under the impression that you and I are at the same point that we were a couple of weeks ago."

"Yeah, well, when someone has a hired goon knock me around, it kind of sticks in my memory."

"I am past that, even if you are not. Besides, we have more pressing matters to discuss."

"I didn't know we were meeting right now," I said. "I don't have the box on me."

"Keep it," he said. "Seems like *my* blackmailer is a step ahead of yours."

Before I could say anything, Vinny turned his head and nodded at Robbie, who reached into the backpack he was holding and pulled out a folded piece of paper. He walked over and handed it to Vinny, who then turned and handed it to me. I unfolded the paper. There was a message, written in all capital letters, stylized so that it would be impossible to tell who sent it just from the handwriting. It said, "Last Year vs. Lincoln, 1/17, you and a friend were chatting before the game. Didn't know you were also posing for a picture, did you? I have the photo and I'm just so torn. What to do . . . what to do . . ." Then, written on the bottom: "Wednesday. Locker 416. $256 and 4 boxes of candy, or I start asking other people for advice."

"Two hundred and fifty-six dollars?" I said. "Odd amount. Are you going to pay it?"

"At the moment, I don't have a choice," Vinny said.

"They're not going to stop once you pay them—you know that, don't you? They'll just ask for more."

"I realize that, yes," he said. "Your concern for my finances is touching, Matthew."

"It's not your finances I'm concerned about, Vincent. You don't think I believe you're here to ask my advice, do you?"

Vinny smiled. "No."

I looked over Vinny's shoulder at Robbie; he was holding a duffel bag.

"For me? You shouldn't have," I said. "I mean that. You really shouldn't have."

Vinny smiled again. "Now, I know doing a drop wasn't part of our original agreement." He pulled a roll of fives out of his pocket and held it out to me but not too far. He wanted me to reach for it. I didn't.

"So why do I deserve to have money thrown at me for such mundane tasks?" I asked.

"You're honest, Matthew. And you're a professional."

"If I'm supposed to be flattered by this, you'll have to compliment me on my eyes first," I said. "How do I know that bag isn't full of stolen exams, and Katie Kondo and her monitors aren't waiting at my locker, ready to slap me in the face with a suspension notice?"

Vinny snapped his fingers, then held his hand open. Robbie gave him the duffel bag. Vinny handed the bag to me, then nodded. I unzipped the bag. There were four boxes of candy and two stacks of five-dollar bills, each held together with a rubber band; one of the stacks had a single dollar bill folded and tucked under the band.

I zipped the bag closed and handed it back to Vinny. He handed it back to Robbie.

"What if I say no?" I asked.

"Well, then, you'd force me to convince you, Matthew."

"Threat?" I asked.

"Let's just say that I'm not the only person with something at stake." His gaze drifted from my face to over my right shoulder. I turned my head. Will was standing there, watching us. He looked angry and defiant but also fearful.

I turned back to Vinny, an expression of disbelief on my face. "What was in that box?" I asked.

"I tell you mine if you tell me yours," Vinny said.

I didn't say anything.

"No?" he said. "I didn't think so. All you need to remember is that the basketball team—more specifically, one particular basketball player—is very important to this school. There's no telling what would happen to this place if faith in that player was somehow betrayed. The word 'riot' comes to mind. People would get hurt. Some more than others." Vinny's eyes shifted back over to Will. I didn't need to look this time.

"That's not on me," I said.

"It is now," Vinny said.

"You can find some other kid to do it."

"I could . . . and maybe the kid I find figures I didn't pay him enough to do the job," Vinny said. "Or maybe he's got a sweet tooth and gets a little hungry, and maybe the duffel bag gets a little lighter before he drops it off."

"Nobody would be stupid enough to mess with you."

"Never underestimate the stupidity of others, Matthew."

"And if I'm still not convinced?" I asked.

Vinny sighed. "Well, then, you'll have to talk to Jacob and Harold."

I looked over at the two hulking guards. They smiled at me. One of them waved.

"I want what I want, Matthew . . . and what I want is for you to do the drop. What condition you are in when you say yes is up to you."

Jenny looked at me, as if daring me to say no, just so she could watch me get roughed up.

"Is this the original?" I asked, holding up the blackmail note.

Vinny nodded.

"Any way I can get a copy?"

Robbie handed Vinny another piece of paper, and he held it out to me. I glanced at both before handing him back the original. I folded up the copy and slipped it into my pocket.

"I'll think about it," I said.

"The drop is tomorrow afternoon. I'll expect an answer first thing tomorrow morning," Vinny said. He looked at me for an extra beat, to let me know that he meant it, and then he turned and walked out. Robbie followed close behind him, but Jenny lingered for a moment.

"You should live up to your principles, Matty-boy, and just say no," she said in a mocking tone. "I want to see Jacob and Harold here knock you around a little. Or a lot."

Jacob and Harold didn't look like they liked Jenny speaking for them, but they kept quiet.

"Hey, Jenny, how long do you think before Vinny realizes that he should've stuck with your sister?" I asked. She clenched her jaw, and the tendons in her neck stood at attention. "What am I saying?" I continued. "He probably already does, because the only thing you appear to be good at is overplaying your hand."

She took a step toward me, her left hand moving behind her toward her waistband, reaching for the squirt gun I assumed was there. "You want to see what else I'm good at, Matty-boy?" she hissed.

I looked over at Jacob, who was looking at Harold, who was already taking a hesitant step toward Jenny. She outranked him, but he had orders from a higher power.

Just as her hand was about to wrap around her squirter, Vinny called out from the hallway. "Jennifer. Time to leave."

Her hand stopped. She took a deep breath, then exhaled slowly. She knew if she popped me now, she might as well squirt herself, too. Kids who don't follow Vinny's orders end up in the Outs, no matter what their "rank." She knew this, but she was still taking a moment to mull it over.

"Hey, lapdog, your master's calling," I said, not able to keep myself from pouring more gas on the fire.

Her hand made a small movement toward her waistband but then stopped again. Harold had taken another step toward her, this one more sure. She turned to him. "Where do you think you're going, you clumsy idiot?" she snarled. He shrugged and smiled. If she was lashing out at him, then she was done with me. As if to prove it, she turned and stomped toward the door.

Jacob shot me a look that managed to be both amused and threatening.

"What can I say?" I said. "I couldn't help myself."

"Next time try," Jacob said, "or the only person who will be able to help you will be the nurse."

The two bruisers each gave me a surprisingly dainty little wave, then walked out.

I turned to see Will's reaction to all of this, but he was already gone.

10

The hallways were full of kids, as they always were in between classes. No Will in sight, but it was easy to figure out where he'd been: he'd left a trail of disappointed people.

"You think he's okay?" one girl asked her friend.

"I wonder what's wrong with him?" another girl said to no one in particular.

The bell rang. Kids filtered into their classrooms. For a moment, I considered doing the same. I had enough heat on me from classmates . . . I didn't need to add any from teachers. But I had a feeling if I let Will go, I'd be letting the first real lead of this case slip right through my fingers.

I caught up to him two hallways later, in a section that led right into a stairwell. There were lockers there but no classrooms. I ducked back around the corner without him seeing me. I could hear his sneakers squeak as he paced. When I heard his steps moving away from me, I snuck a peek. He was walking with his head down, staring at the floor. I heard footsteps echoing through the stairwell at the end of the hall. Will stopped short with a loud squeak. I wasn't sure if it was because of the footsteps on the stairs or because he had spotted me. I held my breath.

"Pete," he said.

From the other end of hall, I heard "Will." The voice belonged to Peter Kuhn, ex-teammate and former tandem superstar on the Franklin Middle School basketball team.

Last winter, the basketball team had been piling up wins, rolling along unbeaten and seemingly unbeatable. Most schools had one player that no one could handle; the Frank had two: Will Atkins and Peter Kuhn. Will had sprouted at an early age and could dominate the low post. Peter hadn't sprouted at all. He was small but wiry, fast, and agile. His court vision was incredible, and he made a lot of passes that looked like optical illusions. He was also deadly from fifteen feet. This presented other teams with a whole host of problems. Have the defense collapse on Will, and Pete would kill you from the outside; contest Pete too much on the perimeter, and he'd just pump it inside to Will. Neither of them was selfish; all they wanted to do was win. And they did . . . until it all fell apart.

There were only five games left in the regular season, and talk had already turned to the state championship tournament. Our involvement was considered a given. The only question was whether we'd run the table or not. Because of Will and Pete, the prevailing opinion was that we would. It was assumed that we'd sweep our last five games and head into the tournament undefeated, the clear favorites to win it all. We were at home, facing Carver Middle School, a cream-puff team. Everyone was already talking about our next game, which was against Colgate, the only team that could possibly provide a challenge to our undefeated season. As so often happens when you're looking too far in front of you, someone creeps up from behind and whacks you in the head.

About five plays into the Carver game, everyone knew something was wrong. Pete wasn't passing to Will. Carver's best defender was covering Pete, which meant that Will was completely open, but Pete refused to pass to him. At first, everyone thought it was a strategy, that our team knew that Carver was planning something to combat Will on the inside . . . all they had to do was trick Pete into passing to him and we'd fall into their trap. But then we'd look at our coach, who was trying frantically to get Pete to pass to Will. Pete wouldn't do it. Instead, he'd pass to Charlie Hutchins, who would promptly turn it over. Or he'd hoist up an off-balance three with a hand or two in his face. When Carver figured out that this wasn't some scheme, they pulled their guy off Will and started double-teaming Pete, forcing turnovers, getting him to make bad passes or off-balance shots.

Will still scored twenty that game, but most of them were on put-backs or the result of hustling after the latest air ball that Pete threw up. It wasn't enough. Carver won by fifteen. Everyone was stunned as they filed out of the gym that day, the same question on everyone's lips: What the heck was up with Pete?

Shortly after the Carver debacle, several kids saw Pete talking to Vinny Biggs. Actually, it was more like arguing. A rumor started to spread: Pete was in with Vinny and had thrown the game. Because Carver was a heavy underdog, the payoff would've been substantial. There was no hard evidence, but it was the best explanation for Pete's performance. People couldn't believe it. Not *Pete*.

Then came the disclosure of Pete's addiction to Pixy Stix, followed rapidly by the revelation that he was stealing cameras from his classmates to pay for that addiction, and suddenly the idea that Pete would throw a game for a big payoff didn't seem so far-fetched.

The basketball team had earlier proved to be a unifying force in a school that was becoming more and more fractured, but all of that was getting wiped out as news about Pete spread. Kids were losing hope that there was anything left at the Frank not tainted by corruption.

Pete rode the pine for the next game. The official word was that he had a pulled hamstring. It might have been more believable if he actually had a limp. That was the Colgate game. Will was able to keep it close. He put up thirty in a losing effort, almost all of it against a fierce double-team. After the game, Pete was thrown off the team. He'd been a mess ever since.

Will fought valiantly for the rest of the season, and

he got his points every game. The problem was that he was surrounded by subpar players. Teams let him score his points, but they didn't let him beat them. We won just two out of the last five games. It was enough to get into the State Tournament. It was also enough to give teams a glimpse of how to beat us. We got bounced in the first round.

The losing didn't affect Will's popularity, though. If anything, it made him even more popular than before. Kids looked up to him. When faced with an impossible task, he wouldn't quit. It's not an exaggeration to say that Will kept hope alive at the Frank; in fact, that might not be giving him enough credit.

When we started the new season, everyone soon realized that the team finally had some decent players to back Will up. Some kids came back taller and more coordinated. There was even a sixth grader who was a hotshot point guard with slick moves, reminiscent of a young Pete. Hope had been restored.

I stole another quick peek around the corner. Will had his back to me. Pete was at the other end of the hallway, facing me. His eyes drifted past Will, but I couldn't tell if he saw me or was just having a hard time focusing. I ducked back.

"What did you give me to hold?" Will yelled.

"What do you mean?"

"What was in the box?"

"Box?" Pete asked. "It was a decorative piece of wood, worth a lot of money. My grand—"

I heard something slam into a locker; by the sound of it, I guessed it was Pete. "Stop lying to me!" Will yelled. "I swear to God, Pete, I still care about you. We were close, man . . . like brothers . . . But I will kill you. Don't think I won't. Melissa got put in the Outs because I trusted you! Now tell me what was in the damn box!"

"I need a little Stix, man . . . just a little . . ."

"Tell me what was in the box!"

"I need some Stix . . . give me some Stix and I'll tell you . . ." Pete's tone had changed. His breathing was shallower; his voice was oily with desperation. "Just one, brother . . . come on . . ."

Will sighed. "What happened to you?" His voice was filled with frustration and pity.

"What happened?" Pete asked. "What *happened*? Don't pretend like you don't know!"

"Shut up."

"NO! *You* don't tell *me* to shut up!" he cried, like a little boy throwing a tantrum. "You hear me? You lost that right! Got it?"

"You're pathetic."

"Yeah, I'm pathetic! That's right, Peter Kuhn is a damn pity case, but Will Atkins, hoo, boy! Will is a frickin' hero! That's the word around school! Have you heard? 'Cause I've heard it! I hear it every damn day!"

There were sounds of a scuffle.

"Tell me what you gave me to hold!" Will spit out through gritted teeth.

"It *was* a box. All right, I admit it. You happy?" Pete cried. "Go ahead and guess what was in it. Go ahead. Three guesses, and then I'll tell you. You want a hint?"

"You little scumba—"

"You want a hint? Here . . . I'll give you a hint. It's worth a lot of money to a lot of different people. Some of them want to pay to make it disappear. And some . . . well, some want to pay to—"

"That's enough," Will said. There were sounds like someone was shaking a shirt that had just come out of the dryer. "I'm through with you, Pete. You hear me? Through."

"Oh, *you're* through with *me*?" Pete said. "No, no . . . *I'm* through with yo— Hey! Ow! OW!"

Will was doing something to Pete, but I didn't want to blow my cover by looking. Whatever it was, it sounded painful.

"If I go down, *you're* going to take the heat," Will said. "All of it. You think it was bad before?"

"They won't— Nobody will—"

"Oh, no? Why? Who are they going to believe: Me? Or some burned-out Stixer like you? You're an ugly footnote to this school's history. That's *it*. And the only thing you'll have to worry about is what'll happen first: you getting thrown out of school or Vinny Biggs putting you in the Outs."

There was a pause. Even the sounds of the struggle stopped. "I knew you were crazy," Will said, "but I didn't think you'd be stupid enough to try and blackmail Vinny."

"Blackmail Vinny? What the hell are you talking about?"

"That's it. Play dumb. And while you're at it, you might as well play sick, too," Will said. "Maybe take a few days off . . . like a hundred and sixty . . ." I heard the meaty sound of two bodies colliding, followed by the metallic *bang!* of one of those bodies hitting a locker.

Then the squeak of Will's sneakers echoed through the stairwell as he walked away.

I peeked around the corner. Pete was sitting on the floor with his back against a locker. His knees were up, with his elbows resting on them. His eyes were closed, and he was wiping his face with the palms of his hands, over and over and over again. Then he stopped, his hands still covering his face. He sat there for a minute, then lifted his head up. I ducked around the corner before he could see me.

I heard him root around in his pockets, then pull something out. From the sound of it, it was his cell phone. I heard him punch in some numbers.

"Yeah, it's me," he said. "So, uh . . . you . . . uh . . . you got any Stix?"

There was a pause.

"No, man . . . You know I'm broke. Come on! I was hoping you could—"

Another pause.

"No . . . My birthday's not for another three months."

There wasn't just a note of desperation in his voice; there was a whole symphony. "Come on, man! You didn't even know that picture existed before I told you!"

My ears perked up. *Picture.*

"Yeah, but what you gave me wasn't enough!"

I could hear yelling coming from the other end of the phone, but I was too far away to hear who it was or what was being said.

"I can't! I don't have it anymore!" Pete yelled back in a loud whisper.

More yelling from the phone.

"I don't know who has it now! You're the ones who took out Melissa . . . and I didn't even know she had it!"

The Thompsons.

"I told you, I don't know who has it now," Pete whined. "I just— I want some Stix. Come on . . . just give me a . . . just a taste and I'll . . . I swear, I'll— Hello? Hello?!?" His phone clattered to the floor. I heard him make a sound in his throat, full of frustration and helplessness. It was more animal than human.

He picked up his phone and started tapping on the keys. Judging by the number of taps, he was texting someone this time. Then he stopped. I thought he might leave, but he didn't; he just sat there, waiting.

I sat waiting, too. There was no point in trying to follow Will at this point. I'd have to pass Pete to do it. Plus, it seemed that the action had shifted from Will to Pete.

After only a couple of minutes, a set of footsteps echoed through the stairwell, then stopped echoing as they entered the hallway. "What do you want?" came a voice, strong, authoritative, feminine, and unmistakable.

"I'm in trouble," Pete whimpered. "I need help."

"What do you want me to do about it?"

"Please don't do *this*."

"Don't do what?" she asked. "Come running every time you call? I already did that. Apparently, I'll always do that, no matter what my better judgment tells me."

"I need your help!"

"I can't, Pete. I can't. Because here's what happens every single time: First you take my help. And you promise you're going to change. Then you end up on another sugar jag, and then *I* end up cleaning up the mess."

"Would you just listen? I need help getting something back that belongs to me."

The girl let out a long sigh. "What is it?" she asked in a voice that didn't want to ask, but did so out of force of habit.

"I can't tell you. You have to trust me."

Her laugh was short and sharp, like a bark from an unfriendly dog. "You make it easy to say no."

"Please?" he pleaded.

"You're kidding, right? Trust you?" she yelled. There was a pause, then she continued, but much quieter. "After everything you've done to me? After everything you've done to yourself?"

"What about what we had? What we still feel for each other?"

"You slimy, little—" She stopped herself before she filled in that space. "I have to go. I shouldn't even be talking to you."

"We liked each other!" he cried.

"I'll give you one deal. That's it."

"Anything . . ."

"Tell me what it's about," she said. "Official. On the record."

"Anything but that," he mumbled.

"Then I can't help you." I could hear her sniffle as she started walking away.

"Wait! You can't!" Pete cried. "I need you!"

No response, just a soft squeak from her sneakers as she left.

"Wait! Wai—" Pete's words turned to sobs. I stood rooted. It was one of the few times in my life when I had no idea what to do next. The voice of the girl, the girl who finally stood up to Pete despite what she still felt for him . . . that voice belonged to Katie Kondo.

When school got out, I went down to Sal's and ordered a root beer, hoping it would help to clear my head. Katie Kondo—the toughest, most no-nonsense hall monitor the school had ever seen—had a soft spot for Peter Kuhn, career criminal and Pixy Stixer. She had talked about cleaning up messes for him, implying that she had bent some rules to do so. My imagination kicked into overdrive, coming up with horrible crimes that Pete could have committed but that we'd never find out about . . . because Katie had orchestrated their cover-ups.

My world no longer made sense. One root beer wasn't going to clear things up, so I ordered three more. I figured that if drinking them didn't work, I could always try hitting myself on the head with the bottles.

When Cynthia walked in, I was so hopped up on sugar, I swear I could hear her heart beat. She spotted me at the bar and headed my way. She was wearing a tan suede jacket and a maroon skirt. Her hair was left wild and free in a sizable Afro. She was stunning, gorgeous, glamorous, and every other variety of flat-out heart-stopping. Two girls at a nearby table stopped chattering for a minute to watch her walk by.

She sat down next to me. Almost immediately, Sal accidentally knocked over a bunch of empty bottles. I gave him a wry smile; he gave me a nervous one back, then scurried off to see if the two girls at the table needed refills.

I saw Cynthia looking at me out of the corner of my eye. "I need to talk to you about—" she started.

"Wait," I interrupted. I slugged down the rest of my third bottle with a twitch and a grimace and reached for the fourth.

"Are you okay?" she asked.

"Yeah . . . Three root beers will do that to a guy."

She reached over and grabbed the last bottle.

"That won't stop me," I said. "I'll order more."

"Shut up. I'm thirsty," she said, then pounded half the bottle in one swallow. She let out a little burp that managed to be both tough and feminine. Then she downed the rest. She put the empty bottle on the bar, then licked her index finger and ran it along the rim, twice. It created a ghostly *whooooo* sound that made Sal looked up from what he was doing. Cynthia used that opportunity to order two more root beers.

"So, what are we drinking to?" she asked after Sal slid the bottles over.

"The deterioration of my imagination," I answered.

"Hopefully not all of it," she said, and gave me a smile that most guys would trade years of detention to see.

We clinked bottles, then took a drink. "Okay, so I'm no detective," she said, "but I'm pretty sure something's bothering you."

"What do you know about the last game Peter Kuhn played in?" I asked, before her smile could distract me any further.

"Peter Kuhn's last game," she repeated, as if she wasn't quite sure she remembered it.

"Yeah, you know . . . the most infamous game in Franklin history? Shouldn't be that hard to remember."

"I know the same as you," she said. "The same as everybody. Pete threw the game to make a quick buck, but Will did everything he could to try and win it anyway."

"How?"

"Pete wouldn't pass to Will. Whenever Pete had the ball, he'd try to drive and shoot or he'd pass it to one of the other players—you know, other than Will. They lost, Pete got caught, and he's been hooked on Pixy Stix ever since."

"Nothing else?" I asked.

"Nope."

"Bull," I said. "You're not a bad liar, but you're not a great one, either. What else did you hear?"

She smiled, as if lying to me had been a test and I had passed it. "Couple of things," she said. "We're there all the time, so of course we hear stuff. I've heard that Pete wasn't the only kid throwing that game. That he had help."

"Who?"

"No one mentioned any names."

"Do you believe it?"

She paused for a moment. "I don't know. It was a bizarre game. Were you there?"

"Yeah, but I had other things going on."

"What kind of other things?" she said with a sly smile on her face.

"Casework. Nothing I can talk about."

"Oh," she said. "Making out with someone under the bleachers?"

"Uhhh . . . no. Why are you so interested?"

"Maybe I want to talk to one of your satisfied customers."

I started sweating, which meant either I had malaria or I just realized that Cynthia was hitting on me. "So, what about the game," I said, trying to get us back on target.

She held her index finger up, then placed it gently on my lips. "Shhh," she said. "I'm not sure I want to talk about the game anymore. I think I found a topic that's more . . . intriguing."

Before she could say anything else, the door opened. When Liz Carling walked in, I knew that fate and karma both hated me. Cynthia must have seen it on my face, because without a word, she turned to see what I was staring at: Liz, framed by the doorway, looking straight at us. Cynthia slowly let her finger fall away from my lips. It didn't matter; Liz had already seen it.

Liz looked at us for a second or two, then cast her eyes to the floor and walked over to a table in the front. Two of her friends came in behind her, giggling and talking. They all sat down. Liz stared at us, as if she didn't want to but couldn't help it. Liz's friends were still chatting and laughing. When they tried to include Liz, they noticed that she wasn't listening to them. They followed the line of her stare until all three of them were looking at Cynthia and me. Her friends' smiles disappeared.

"You okay?" Cynthia whispered to me. "Matt?"

"Yeah . . . sorry . . . I'm all right. But I have to . . . uh . . ."

"Yeah, I know," she said. "Go ahead."

I stood up and walked to the far end of the bar, feeling like a baby giraffe who had just learned to walk. I sat down on one of the stools.

Liz stood up from her table and walked over. She sat on the stool to my right. Her friends watched us.

"Matt," she said.

"Hey, Liz. Taking a break from chess?" I asked. I tried to sound casual, but I felt stiff and unnatural.

"It's okay, Matt. I know it's just business."

"It's just business."

"I know. I just said that." A wicked smile spread across her face. "There's no way that girl would be talking to you if it were anything but."

"Ow."

"Don't try to trade barbs with a chess master. We know your moves before you do."

"Oh, so you're a chess master now?" I asked. "Where's your robe?"

"At the dry cleaner's," she said. She looked over at Cynthia. "You should go. Your client looks like she's getting restless. And she's not the type to wait around for someone . . . not even the great Matt Stevens." She was still trying to joke, but there was something odd and forced about her tone.

"You anxious to get rid of me?" I was kidding, but it didn't really sound like I was, to either of us.

She took a deep breath. "No, Matt, it's just . . ." She paused.

The words "it's just" hung in the air, foreshadowing worse things to come.

"It's just what?" I asked, though I wasn't sure I wanted to know.

"It's just that . . . I feel like I'm holding you back."

I laughed. "From what?"

She peered over my shoulder at Cynthia. I started to turn, when Liz hissed at me. "Stop! She'll know we're talking about her."

"Yeah . . . right . . . she'd have no idea otherwise."

Liz smiled and shook her head. "She just smiled at me, and even I got warm and tingly."

"Look, it's just business," I said. "She's the head cheerleader, for crying out loud."

"I know, Matt. It's not that . . . it's just—" She paused.

"Stop saying 'it's just' and then stopping."

"Sorry. It's just that I don't think either of us can really commit to anything right now. I have my chess, you have your business . . ."

"No. That's bull," I said. "We've had these for a while and they've never gotten in the way."

She blushed and looked down at the bar. "We've only just been friends before," she said, barely above a whisper.

I felt my cheeks get warm, and the back of my scalp start to tingle. "Well, what do you think we'll be after this?"

"I don't know." She paused. "Look, I know your talking to her is just business. And I know you have to talk to girls all the time, and some of those girls are going to fall for you . . ."

"You give me too much credit."

"I know." She smiled, looked at me for a second, and then dropped her eyes. "It's because I like you."

"I like you, too . . . but that doesn't seem to be working in my favor right now."

"I just think that right now both of us need our freedom."

"Liz, I—"

"I tried calling you. I wanted to talk about this privately. I didn't expect to see you here with—" She stopped.

"With Cynthia," I said, finishing it for her.

"No. Yes." She ran her hand over her face. "It's not Cynthia."

"But it is."

She sighed. "I just . . . I don't know, Matt. It is, and it isn't. Look, you and I have something really special, and I don't want to ruin it."

"So you're ending it?" I asked. "How does that make sense?"

"I just don't want to end up hating you."

"Well, what if I hate you for doing this?"

"You'll recover. You're built that way."

"Liz—"

"Stop," she said and slid off her bar stool. "You can't change my mind on this. And trust me, if she's going to be your client, you'll be glad that you're rid of me." She tried to smile, to show me that she could tease me about other girls, just like "one of the boys," but her smile looked more like a grimace.

"Liz—"

She put her hand over my mouth to stop me, in a gesture that resembled the one she just saw Cynthia do to me.

"Good-bye, Matt." She gave me a soft kiss on the cheek. My mind was searching for something to say, something to make her change her mind, but she didn't give me time. She walked over to her friends and said something. They nodded sympathetically. She gave them a little wave good-bye and then slipped out the door.

Cynthia walked up behind me. "Are you okay?" she asked.

"Yeah. Sure."

"Really?"

"You're a client now, so even if I wasn't, I wouldn't tell you. You'd expect a discount."

"I'm sorry, Matt." She put her hand on my shoulder.

It was a simple gesture that caused a complex range of emotions: guilt, longing, happiness, self-loathing, and just a touch of anger.

"Why?" I asked. "You have nothing to be sorry about." I turned to face her. "This was about Liz and me, not you."

She looked me dead in the eyes; her gaze never wavered. "I know. I'm sorry because even though you're hurting right now, I'm glad."

"Glad?"

"Yes. When I'm interested in someone, I prefer that they're unattached."

She blushed. As tough as she was, laying herself bare like that was a dicey proposition. I looked over at Sal, to see if I was imagining it. His facial expression made it obvious that I wasn't. He looked proud, envious, and incredulous all at the same time.

"I have to go," she said. "School tomorrow . . . I'll see you." She gave me a light kiss on the cheek, opposite the one Liz had kissed, as if she were leaving it for comparison. She walked out the door. I turned to watch her. When she was gone, I looked at Sal again. I couldn't tell if he wanted to give me a congratulatory hug or a punch in the mouth.

$\mathcal{I}$ had to walk my bike home from Sal's. There was no way I could drive in my condition.

Cynthia Shea, head cheerleader and overall knockout, had kissed me. I should've been happy. I should've been flying home instead of walking . . . but I couldn't get Liz out of my mind.

Most guys would think I was nuts or that maybe I had taken one too many dodgeballs to the head. From a looks standpoint, they'd be right. Liz was beautiful, no question, but Cynthia was at a level seldom seen in middle school. She was dangerous-at-intersections gorgeous.

But looks didn't matter. Okay, they mattered a little—maybe more than a little—but they didn't mean *everything*. And Cynthia wasn't just one-dimensional, a cardboard cutout with a pretty face. She was smart, and funny, and fierce.

But Liz and I just clicked. We'd always clicked. There was no other way to explain it.

That being said, Liz had just sandbagged me with the "Let's just be friends" conversation, when our "Let's be more than friends" relationship had barely even started. It was like crash-landing a plane when you'd only gotten two feet off the ground.

Cynthia was the full package, but I couldn't shake the feeling that if I wasn't *necessary* to her, she wouldn't know my name. She had an agenda, and I felt like she was using me as a means to an end.

When I got home, I saw my mom's car in the driveway. I was pretty sure that she had a restaurant shift that night, and seeing as how it was now an hour past the point when she should have left for work, it meant that she had quit, had been fired, or was taking a more relaxed attitude toward arrival times.

I noticed an expensive German sedan parked opposite the house. It didn't really fit in with the other cars on our street. It looked like an honor society president sitting in detention. It took me a moment, but then I recognized the car . . . it was the same one that dropped Kevin and Liz off at school every morning.

I walked to the back door, the one by the kitchen. I started to open the screen door when I heard the yelling.

"I'm trying to help!" Mr. Carling shouted.

"I know!" my mom yelled back.

"So why are you making it so hard for me?"

"Because I know *why* you want to help."

I leaned closer to the door as their yelling transitioned into talking.

"No, you don't," he said. "You think you do—"

"No, I know I do," she said. "You're helping so you can prove to me that you were right. So you can shove my nose in it. I made a bad decision. There. I said it. Are you happy now?"

"No, I'm not, damn it! I'm not happy! And I don't care about that! About any of it, for Chrissakes! Will you just listen to me for one second?!?"

I opened the door and walked inside. "*I'll* listen to you for one second," I said. "Several, if you need a little more time."

Mr. Carling's face was about two inches away from my

mom's; he had a firm grip on her shoulders. He let go and backed off. It looked bad, but Mom didn't look worried, not in the least. She looked more confused.

"Matt?"

"Mom . . . Mr. Carling."

Mr. Carling just stood there, trying to decide what to do with his hands. Putting them in his pockets were his first and sixth choices.

He was wearing a suit that was worth two months of groceries for my mom and me. He was good-looking in a "I used to be more good-looking" kind of way. He opened his mouth to speak, realized he wasn't sure what to say, and closed his mouth without saying a word.

"You were grabbing and yelling at my mom in our kitchen," I said. "The least you could do is say hello."

"Matt. Watch it." My mom tried to sound stern, but I could tell she was playing defense.

"Watch what?" I asked. "And be specific, so I know what to look for."

"Your mom and I were discussing her future," Mr. Carling said. He was trying to regain the upper hand by putting on the arrogant, domineering identity he usually wore. It didn't seem to fit him at the moment.

"I was late for work and Mr. Carling had to come look for me," my mom said.

"Didn't he think to call first?" I asked.

"He did. I didn't answer the phone."

"But you let him in the house."

"Matt, I am really not in the mood for this."

"Well, what are you in the mood for?" I asked. "Me? I'm in the mood for an explanation that makes even a little bit of sense."

Mr. Carling's face broke into an odd little smile. "You let him talk to you this way?" he asked, but there was nothing accusatory in the way he said it. The arrogant tone was gone; he sounded more impressed and amused. I looked at my mom, who looked like she was trying not to laugh. It was my turn to be confused.

"I should go," Mr. Carling said before I had a chance to ask another question. "And, uh . . . this is your final warning, Kathy," he said, trying to sound angry. It just sounded fake. "Do it again, and you're fired. You hear me?" My mom was still trying not to laugh as she nodded yes.

Mr. Carling left, slamming the door behind him, but even that seemed fake.

"Okay," I said, "now you've really lost me."

"Seems pretty cut-and-dried to me," she said, making a concerted effort to squelch her smile.

"You want to talk about it?" I asked.

"No. You?"

"What do you think?"

"I think you want to talk about it," she said, "but you're bound by our agreement. You're not ready to tell me what's going on in your world, but you want to know what's going on in mine."

A while back, my mom and I made an agreement: I agreed not to ask her about how her odd relationship with Mr. Carling was affecting her life; she agreed not to ask me what was going on at school that was causing me to get into fights. It was an uneasy truce, and neither one of us was very comfortable with it . . . but we kept it. However, I was getting the feeling that this truce had an expiration date, and it was rapidly approaching. It was already starting to smell bad.

"You're right," I said. "I'm not ready to talk about it. It's just that I didn't expect you to bring your secrets home with you."

"Neither did I."

"Is it about Dad, and why he left?"

She looked away from me. "There's no way to answer that," she said.

"A simple yes or no will do."

"Not in this case it won't."

"Just pick the one that more closely fits, then," I said.

"Why? It won't do you any good. You won't know any more about it."

"I don't know anything now, so what's the difference?" I asked.

"It's worse to think you know something . . . you make all sorts of false assumptions when you think you know something."

"So what should I assume about Mr. Carling being here?" I asked.

"Nothing."

"You expect me to buy that?"

"What's going on at school?" she countered. "Does it have something to do with all the 'jobs' you take and all that money you keep bringing home?"

My eyes got wide.

"Yeah . . . didn't think I knew about that, did you? I swear Matt, I know I'm busy, but I'm trying not to be insulted by how clueless you think I am."

"I don't think you're clueless," I mumbled.

"What?"

"I said, I don't think you're clueless."

She took a deep breath. "I know."

We looked at each other. I felt the anger drain out of me, like it was air and I was a tire with a slow leak.

"So what do we do now?" I asked.

"We could tell each other everything."

"Okay," I said. "You first."

She smiled. I smiled. Even when we didn't really trust each other, at least we could still crack each other up. "Any other ideas?" I asked.

"Are you hungry?" she asked.

"Kind of."

"You want to go into town? Get something to eat?"

I didn't say anything. Walking around town was something that made us feel closer together, and closer to my dad's memory. I wasn't sure I was in the state of mind to feel that right now.

"Yeah," she said, reading me like a one-page picture book. "Me, neither."

"I have some homework I need to get to," I said.

"Yeah . . . of course . . . Listen, I should probably check in at the restaurant, see if I can help out. You know, at least try to keep my job," she said.

"Right. Yeah."

"Okay, well, I'll see you tonight." She grabbed her purse and headed for the door. "Don't wait up."

"Yeah, okay."

She looked at me. Her eyes started to get damp, but she left before the dam broke. I sat at the kitchen table, listening to our decrepit car drive away.

The next morning, my mom and I met in the kitchen. We didn't talk, just sipped our beverages.

I almost told her everything. I wasn't sure if it was the fact that I was exhausted or that my mom's face was puffy, maybe from crying. All I knew was that I was tired of this distance between us, tired of not knowing and not telling. I wanted it over.

She must've sensed something was up with me, because whenever I looked at her, she had a strange expression on her face. It was sincere but also a little smiley. I couldn't tell if it was caring or pre-triumphant because she could tell that I was inches away from cracking.

I opened my mouth, not sure how I was going to begin.

"Stop," she said, before I could even get started. "Don't tell me anything right now." She took a sip of coffee.

"I don't know what you're talking about," I said with mock arrogance. "I was nowhere near about to crack and tell you everything right now while sipping my orange juice."

She smiled. "You shouldn't. Not now. If you tell me, then I have to tell you, and then neither one of us is going to get to where we need to go today."

"So . . . ?"

She smiled. "Tomorrow's Thursday. I have the night off. We'll have a party. You and me. We'll hang out, eat something good that's bad for us, and then, when the clock strikes nine, we'll air our dirty laundry. Sound good?"

I smiled. My heart tripped a couple of times just thinking about talking about Vinny, the Outs, and everything else that went on at school. "I don't think it's ever going to sound good," I said, "but it does sound right."

"That'll have to do."

"Amen."

She wrapped me up in a big hug. When we unclasped, she grabbed the side of my head and planted a big kiss on my forehead. "Ahhh, *mio figlio*," she said. *"Ti amo . . . ti amo!"* She smiled at me, one of her thousand-watt ones, and pinched my cheeks. Before I could ask her what she had said, and in what language, she was already on her way to the bathroom to shower and get ready for work.

I figured it out an hour later, as I was walking to school. She was speaking Italian. The answer just popped into my head, and for some reason I knew it was right. But why was my mom suddenly speaking to me in Italian? I had no idea what to make of it.

When I got to school, my brain started ticking off the names of the kids I didn't want to run into: Liz, Vinny, Jenny Finnegan. Cynthia I wasn't sure about. Part of me wanted to see her more than anyone else in the world; the other part of me was scared to death of her. I was so preoccupied, I almost ran into the girl in front of me.

"I'm sorry," I said. "I didn't see you. My mind was orbiting Satur—"

She turned around, and for a moment, I didn't

recognize her. Her blond hair stuck out like uncooked spaghetti. Her skin was pale and blotchy, and there were small clusters of pimples on her forehead and right cheek. Her eyes were still bright blue, but their gaze was more piercing and uncomfortable than attractive. Her body was barely visible under her baggy, shapeless clothes.

"Melissa?" I said.

Before I could say anything else, her eyes filled up with tears. I reached out for her, to try to stop her from running away, but she turned and ran off anyway.

"Melissa!" I called after her. She threaded her way through the hall like a person afraid to touch anyone. Kids glanced at her as she passed but didn't pay her much attention. By the time the shock wore off, she was gone. I wasn't sure if I had just witnessed a reminder of my duty or an omen of my future.

I trudged over to my locker. Cynthia was already there, waiting, leaning against it in a pose that mirrored Melissa's from a couple of days ago. You can tell your life has taken a drastic turn when you see a gorgeous cheerleader waiting for you and you're not sure it's a good thing. I approached her cautiously. She saw me coming and straightened up.

"I just wanted to apologize again for yesterday," she

said. She looked at me, then cast her eyes to the floor. "I didn't mean to come between you and Liz."

"You didn't."

"Are you sure?"

"No."

"Well, good, then," she said, and smiled. "Because I'm not sure I'm sorry." She took a step closer to me. I noticed for the first time that she was a half-inch taller than me, adding to the list of her intimidating attributes. She leaned toward me, her lips as close to mine as they could get without actually touching. "In fact, I know I'm not."

My heart thumped in my chest. "Interesting," I said, my voice only cracking on every other syllable. "I suppose it's only a matter of time before I figure out your angle."

Her expression changed to one of confusion, but she stood her ground. "What do you mean?"

"I'm sure there's a reason why you've decided to stand this close to me, but I don't think it has anything to do with my charm."

She pulled her head back but only a little. "You really should have more confidence in yourself," she said.

"Yeah, well, past experience and the last couple of days beg to differ."

As if on cue, Vinny, Jenny, and three of Vinny's goons came around the corner. "Oh, my," Vinny said. "Looks like we're interrupting something special."

Cynthia took a step away from me and turned to Vinny. "I don't think we've met," she said.

"Vincent Biggio," he said, holding out his hand. Cynthia shook it politely. "And we have, my dear, but I wouldn't expect you to remember. I was a different boy then."

"Different how?" she asked.

He smiled. "In every way possible. Now, if you will excuse us, Matthew and I have a matter to discuss."

"I like discussions," she said in a way that managed to be innocent and defiant at the same time.

Vinny chuckled. "You and I met at the beginning of last year. One of the cheerleaders—I believe her name was Gretchen—made a rather annoying habit of calling me a big fat pig whenever she got the chance. She made the mistake of doing that in your presence once, and you proceeded to 'rip her a new one,' as they say. This, even though she was a year ahead of you and a bit of a 'queen bee.'"

"I know what it's like to be picked on for something you can't control," she said.

Vinny looked her up and down. I didn't like it. "Yes, well, it seems as if you've managed nicely. Anyway, I've always been grateful, which is why I'll say to you politely, please leave."

"And if I don't?" she asked.

I looked at her, confused as to where she was going with this.

Vinny chuckled again. "Then Michelle will ask. But I'm afraid she's not as nice as I am." One of the goons behind Vinny took a step forward. She looked like the only thing that she used her head for was cracking walnuts.

"It's okay," I said to Cynthia. "Talking to the likes of Vinny is part of my job description."

"I'm insulted, Matthew," he said. "You should know that there are no 'likes of me.' I'm one of a kind."

Cynthia shot me a look like she didn't want to leave me alone. I gave her a little smile that tried to say that I would be fine, but I'm not sure it did. Maybe because I wasn't sure I would be.

"All right," she said, even though she didn't look happy about it. "I'll see you later." She shot a look at Vinny that seemed to say that she'd *better* see me later.

"Why, Matthew," he said, when Cynthia was finally

out of sight, "I do believe you're stepping up in the world."

"You couldn't expect my charms to be a secret for long. Either that or she has an undisclosed head injury."

"Yes, well, cheerleading is a dangerous sport," he said. "She's feisty. It's been a while since anyone's quasi-threatened me."

"Is there something you want," I asked, "or are you just here to interrupt my climb up the social ladder?"

"Time for you to earn your money."

"I haven't said yes yet."

"No need for you to go to the trouble," Vinny said. "I've already said yes for you." He waved his right hand in a casual gesture. Harold stepped forward and shoved the duffel bag into my locker, then gave me a little wink as he stepped back.

"There's going to be a fire drill after lunch," Vinny said, "before fifth period. Before the alarm goes off, you need to put that bag in locker number 416. It will be open. After you put the bag in, spin the lock, then leave. Do not hang around. Do not try to catch whoever is doing this."

"You don't want to know who it is?"

"I'll find out soon enough, but today is not that day. He or she can watch the locker all day long. And they can pick up the bag whenever they think the coast is clear. They don't have to do it today, or tomorrow, or even next week. They can wait until whenever. And I'm assuming they'll be patient. That's all right. I can be patient, too." A smile crept across his face. It was the smile of someone who savors the destruction of his enemies.

"Seems a little early to give me the stash, no?" I asked. "Are you sure you trust me?"

Vinny laughed. "Don't screw this up, Matthew. I would hate to put you in the Outs over such a mundane task."

Vinny and his goons left. I opened the locker door, grabbed the bag, and unzipped it. Inside were the same contents as yesterday: $256 and four boxes of candy. I zipped the bag back up, closed my locker door, and spun the lock. I leaned my head against the door and looked down at the ground. This felt wrong. Very, very wrong. Then again, that was just stating the obvious. Has performing a blackmail drop ever felt right?

14

$\mathscr{I}$ tried to get through the rest of my classes, but I was too distracted. I was nervous and full of dread, like someone who walks on-stage to perform a piano concerto and suddenly remembers that he never actually learned how to play the piano. I kept making trips back to my locker, to make sure the bag was still there. If someone stole it before I made the drop, I'd just squirt *myself* in the pants and dance the hula through the halls.

As if that wasn't keeping my boxers in a bunch, I kept seeing Liz. It was almost as if she was haunting me. I'd look down a hallway crowded with kids and her face would just appear, somewhere in the back. She'd catch my eye, then look away. A second later, she'd be gone.

By the time lunch rolled around, I was in no mood for anyone. All I wanted to do was sit alone and brood. Poor Matt Stevens, full of melancholy and bologna, alone in a world full of criminals. By the time Kevin sat down across from me, I was ready to write an epic poem in my own honor.

"You're determined to keep bending your luck until it breaks," he said.

"If you have a better idea of what I should've done, considering my options, I'm all ears."

He leaned in, his face pulled in tight to show how serious he was. "If something goes wrong, he's going to come down on you like a ton of Salisbury steaks."

"I believe the saying is 'like a ton of bricks.'"

"Have you tried the Salisbury steak here?" Kevin said. "They make bricks feel like down pillows."

I smiled, but there wasn't much behind it. "So, is this a setup?"

Kevin gave the question some thought. "No," he finally answered, "not in a traditional sense. It's not like Vinny's absolutely sure something's going to happen at the drop and he wants you to bear the brunt of it."

"No?"

"No. He's only partially sure."

"Hey, thanks for stopping by," I said. "You've really brightened up my day."

"Listen, from what I hear, Vinny wants this to go smoothly. And the reason he chose you is because, if something does happen, he figures you've got a pretty good chance of finding a way out of it."

"Nice to hear."

"The other side of the coin is that if something happens and you *can't* find a way out, well . . . let's just say Vinny won't exactly be blowing through boxes of tissues."

"Not as nice to hear, but not exactly a surprise," I said. "You think he's a pro?"

"The blackmailer?" Kevin asked, then shook his head. "Probably not. How many kids are? I just hope he doesn't show up at the drop."

"He may not be a pro," I said, "but judging from his note, I don't think he's stupid, either. He might be expecting some coverage from Vinny."

"He might. He might also show up just to pop you and send a message."

"Thanks," I said. "Thanks a lot."

"You want me to pray for you?" he asked.

"Do you know any prayers?"

"I know a few dirty limericks."

"Yeah," I said. "Unfortunately, I know the same ones."

"Seriously, Matt . . . do you need backup?"

I smiled. "That's a dumb question and you know it. Of course I need backup. The problem is, I need my backup backed up too far to do any good."

"Well," he said, standing up, "it was nice knowing you."

"Yeah, I'm sure it was," I said. "I wish I could say the same in return."

After the bell rang, I sat at my table, waiting for everyone else to file out of the caf. When I was the only kid left, I stood up and walked out into the hallway. Kids with the next lunch period started to trickle in past me. I barely noticed them.

I walked over to my locker, grabbed the bag, then started making my way to the drop-off point. The hallways were deserted. I could hear the muffled sound of classroom activities behind the closed doors as I passed. The school day was going on without me; I just hoped that wouldn't be a permanent arrangement.

Locker 416 was at one end of the main hallway, the longest, widest corridor in the school. Classrooms flanked the locker on both sides, with a couple more across the hall. I stood in front of it, feeling very small and exposed, like a squirrel in the middle of an empty highway. I looked right, then left, to see if anyone was coming. I repeated this motion a few times, but I wasn't obsessive about it. I'm pretty sure I kept it under fifty.

Finally, after I had made myself good and nauseated, I stepped closer to the locker. I flicked my finger under the handle. The trigger snapped up immediately. The door swung open. I stepped back and checked the hallway three more times. No one was there. I shoved the bag into the locker, shut the door, and was about to spin the lock when I heard footsteps behind me.

"Well, what do we have here?" It was Katie Kondo.

I closed my eyes and took a deep breath. "We have a kid . . . that's me," I said, "in front of a locker . . . that's this." I rapped my knuckles on the locker a couple of times. "Any other questions?"

"Get your hands off that lock," she said.

"Why? Afraid you forgot the combination?"

"What did you say?"

"You heard me."

Katie laughed, but it was an abrasive sound. "You think I'm here to pick up what you're dropping off?"

"I think it's odd that you know I'm dropping something off."

"Really. Well, here's a little newsflash for you: Someone finally got sick of your act, Stevens. Now, hands up, and step away from the locker."

I started to put my hands up but then quickly brought them back down and spun the dial, locking it. "Whoops!" I said.

Katie shoved me aside, then spun the lock back and forth in a purposeful way. The latch went up with no resistance. The door swung open, and the duffel bag fell out at her feet. She picked it up, unzipped it, and looked inside. "Care to explain this?" she asked.

"I was just about to ask you the same thing," I replied. "So you just happened to have the combination to this specific locker, huh?"

"Something on your mind, Stevens?" she snarled.

"Yeah. I'm just wondering what you're going to spend the money on."

Her face went red. She slammed her forearm against

my throat and rammed me against the locker. "Accuse me of being crooked. Go ahead. You might wake up in the nurse's office, if you wake up at all."

She let go of me. I didn't rub my throat, even though it hurt like hell. I didn't want to give her the satisfaction.

"Hope you enjoy your week in detention," she said.

"Like hell I will. On what charge?"

"Well, for starters, shouldn't you be in class? And don't go trying to use one of those phony hall passes, because it's not going to work."

I looked at the clock behind Katie. The fire alarm was going to ring any second.

"Who tipped you off?" I asked.

"That's the least of your problems."

"Actually, you're wrong on both counts," I said, trying to keep calm. "I think *we* have been set up. We have to get out of here."

"What's this 'we' stuff, huh? You're the only one I see in the hot seat, Stevens."

"Then you need a better thermometer. Come on, Katie! We have to get out of here!" I scanned the hallway, looking for the most likely spot for an ambush to come from. There were only about a thousand of them.

"You helped my sister, Matt . . . no doubt. But your goodwill is all used up."

I gave a quick look over Katie's shoulder. She must have been a little spooked because she turned her head to see what I was looking at. I used that moment to reach down and grab the duffel bag. I was almost able to rip it out of her hand, but she tightened her grip at the last second.

"Hey!" she yelled.

She yanked the strap, pulling me toward her, then grabbed my right wrist. I did a little under-and-over move with my hand, breaking her grip and grabbing her wrist all in one smooth motion. Before she could react, I pulled her toward me. I lifted my left forearm, and her face ran right into it. I was getting us out of there, even if I had to knock her unconscious to do it.

One small problem: My forearm smash hurt my arm much more than it did her face. She looked more surprised than hurt when the blood started trickling out of her nose. Before I knew what was happening, I was slammed chest-first onto the floor, with my right arm shoved painfully into my solar plexus. She was leaning her weight into my face. Through one watery eye, I could see the duffel bag about six feet away from us down the hall.

"You're going to feel a lot of pain from this day forward, Matt. And hopefully, in a couple of years, you'll regain the use of your right arm."

The squirt gun blasts came in quick succession: one-two. *Pow pow.* I felt the grip on my arm go slack. My face had been squished against the floor, and it took a moment for the wateriness of my eyes to clear up. When they did, I saw Katie Kondo lying there with a giant wet spot on the front of her pants and Tim and Tina Thompson walking toward us, each holding a giant soaker.

Katie was breathing heavily. Her eyes were glazed, filled with shock and panic. "I'm wet. I'm wet. I'm wet!"

"Don't worry, sweetie," Tina purred, "you're about to have a little company."

Tim ran over to me and started to pick me up off the floor with one hand; his other hand still gripped the huge soaker.

I had one shot. I made it count.

Whap!

I hit him in the most sensitive of male areas. He went down, hard. His giant soaker clattered across the floor. I picked it up and pointed it at Tina. She started firing at me. I slid out of the way and fired back at her; not aiming, just random shots. I missed. I started pumping the soaker to build up more pressure.

Tina stopped firing and picked up the duffel bag. "Tim!" she cried. The panic was starting to set in. "Tim! Get up!"

"Cheap . . . shot," Tim said in between gasps and coughs.

"Yeah," I yelled as I pumped, "I'm going to have a tough time sleeping tonight."

He stumbled to his feet and started running off as best he could. Tina took off with the duffel bag in the other direction. I fired a couple more shots at her, but she was out of range. I thought about chasing them, but I had other things to deal with.

"Wet!" Katie yelled as she walked quickly down the hall, looking for a place to hide.

I ran up to her. "Run!" I yelled.

"I'm wet! I'm WET!"

"I know! Shut up and ru—!"

The fire alarm rang.

Before we could get very far, kids started pouring out

of the classrooms. They saw us and froze. We tried to move, but there was nowhere to go. The idea that there might actually be a fire was forgotten; the only thing that mattered was that the great Katie Kondo, chief hall monitor, had a giant wet spot on her pants. And fire or no fire, the kids were going to send her to the Outs in style.

"PEE-PEE PANTS! PEE-PEE PANTS!" The chant filled the hallway.

I wanted her to fight. I wanted to help her, even after all the crap she'd put me through. But I had no idea how.

Then she did something strange. She closed her eyes and took a deep breath, then pursed her lips and let the air out slowly. She opened her eyes. Her face was calm and expressionless. She gazed straight ahead, not out of fear or panic but in silent defiance. She started walking, and as she did, the still-chanting crowd backed out of her way.

She was about halfway out when she stopped. She looked around, then made a quick, aggressive move . . . arms up, like she was going to throw a punch. The crowd flinched, as if everyone hiccuped all at the same time. They tried to chant and yell even louder, to make up some of the intensity they had lost, but you could tell they were forcing it.

Katie started walking forward again, and the crowd parted to let her through. No one wanted to get too close to her. They were trying to intimidate her, but it wasn't working . . . because she was still *waaaay* too intimidating. At best, it was a draw.

But she was done as chief hall monitor. As defiant as she was, I was pretty sure she knew it. No one would respect her authority now. She had lost the battle, but watching her stride off, I wondered whether she was actually out of the war.

Katie Kondo was now in the Outs. On the list
of things that I thought were going to happen that day,
this ranked right after the Foo Fighters playing a concert
in the cafeteria. It was obvious that everyone else in the
school felt the same way. Kids were reveling in the news,
not because they hated Katie and wanted to see her taken
down but because it was the biggest event since Nikki
Fingers landed in the Outs.

I walked the hallways for an hour or so, feeling sick to
my stomach, listening to the news bounce off the walls. As

usual, most of the stories weren't even half right. I didn't intend to end up at Katie's office, but apparently that's where my feet directed me. The door was open a crack. I pushed it open wider, but only enough so I could slip in.

There was someone sitting in Katie's chair, but the back was turned to the door so I couldn't see who it was. The chair started to swivel around. I tensed to jump, thinking it might be an assassin. It wasn't. It was Melanie Kondo, Katie's little sister. Melanie and I had gotten into a fairly serious scrape a couple of weeks ago. I hadn't seen or talked to her since.

"Matt," she said. She hadn't liked me the last time I saw her, and it didn't look or sound like her opinion had changed.

"Mel."

"Come to gloat?"

"No. You?"

"Are you trying to tick me off?" she growled.

"No, but apparently I don't have to try. It just comes naturally."

She smiled a little, then seemed to regret it. She paused before she spoke again. "You were there when Katie went down," she said.

"Yeah."

"How did it happen?"

"I was there on a job. She showed up unannounced."

"What job?"

"That's not something I feel like talking about right now," I said.

Melanie made an unhappy face that I was well familiar with. "Is there anything else?" she asked.

I told her everything about the scene: the Thompsons' well-timed appearance, the fire alarm, the rush of kids, and her sister's response as she went into the Outs. She listened without interrupting; her expression remained neutral, as if I were giving her an oral report about Denmark instead of a blow-by-blow description of how her sister met her end. When I was finished, she stared at me for a moment, then swiveled her chair around so she could look out the window.

"So what do you want?" she asked. "Why'd you come here?"

"I don't know," I said. "Listen, Katie and I almost never saw eye to eye. Neither have you and I—"

"But?"

"But Katie was a good hall monitor. With her out of

the picture, I wonder how this whole school is going to hold together."

"Yeah, you and me both. So, why did you say you were there again?"

"I didn't."

She eyed me suspiciously, then sighed. "And I don't have the authority to make you."

"I wasn't going to say anything, but no . . . no, you don't."

"What if I did?"

"Is this a possibility or a hypothetical?"

"Both. There's a void that needs filling," she said, "and the principal is eyeing me for the 'honor.'"

She didn't look happy about it.

"Your sister's pants aren't even dry yet, and you're taking her place?"

"If the school administration has their way, yes. We Kondos have a legacy as hall monitors."

"Uh-huh. Isn't that going be a little tough, in light of the events from a couple of weeks ago?" I asked.

"You mean the fact that I popped Nikki Fingers?"

"And then gave her sister, Jenny, a black eye and a fat lip. Yup. That'd be what I meant."

She smiled a little, as if she knew she shouldn't enjoy

the memory of messing up Jenny's face but just couldn't help herself. "They don't know about it."

"Excuse me?"

"The administration. Katie never told them. It was her last gift to me."

I sat down. I was having a hard time following the conversation and standing at the same time.

"Katie cooked the books," she continued. "Made it look like Jenny got in with the wrong crowd and picked a fight with the nearest hall monitor."

"You."

"Me."

"So you didn't get suspension?"

She shook her head. "Sick days. That's what's on record. Katie spread the word that I was suspended. Nobody knows."

"And now nobody cares . . . I didn't think she had it in her."

"Neither did I."

"And you were okay with it?"

"Did I have a choice?" she said. "Katie just did it. Maybe she wanted to keep me from tarnishing the Kondo name. Or maybe she just felt an obligation to me . . . I've been looking through her books. She broke a lot of 'laws' as chief, just to give some kids a second chance, sometimes a third."

My mind immediately went to Pete Kuhn, but I wasn't sure if it was my place to talk about him. "Doesn't seem possible," I said.

"But she didn't like you."

"That sounds more like her. So, what are you going to do?"

She sighed. "I don't know."

"Do you want the job?"

"I'm not sure," she said. "Gerry Tinsdale is pretty excited about it."

"Tinsdale? Oh boy . . ."

"You don't think he's up for it?"

"I think he thinks he's up for it. I also think he thinks he's doing a good job now. Gerry needs to be introduced to the concept of reality."

She smiled again, as if she were glad to hear confirmation of what she already suspected.

"I see now what she was trying to do," she said. "I see why this was so important to her. I know what her plans were, why she lived the way she did, made the decisions that she made. She was unsure of herself, unsure of her beliefs, but only in private. In public, she was always decisive, always sure. I don't know if I could be that." She paused. "I'm not sure I'm up to it."

Her words hung there. I wasn't an expert on Melanie Kondo, so there was no way for me to tell her what tasks she was or wasn't up to. All I knew was that in one little conversation, my opinion of her had done a complete one-eighty.

Just then the door opened, and Gerry Tinsdale walked in. He was sixty-five pounds of sneering petulance, and, by my estimate, twenty of those pounds were his badge and clothes.

"Matt Stevens," he said, as if my name tasted like cough syrup. "What are you doing dirtying up one of my chairs?"

"From what I understand," I said, "they're not your chairs yet."

His ears started to turn a nice shade of crimson, like a ripe pomegranate. "This is the hall monitors' office. In here, if I say it's my chair, then you damn well—"

"He's here because I asked him to be," Melanie said, interrupting him.

"Great," he said, trying to recover. "Now he can leave because I asked him to leave."

"I'm not finished with him," Melanie said.

"Tell me why that's even a factor in this discussion," he said, a fat smile planted on his skinny face. "Maybe you should take a *sick day*—you know, to think it over."

Melanie's jaw tightened, and her eyes narrowed in a way that looked instantly familiar to me. Normally, her resemblance to Katie was hard to see, but it appeared as if Gerry had just found the recipe for bringing the Katie out of her. He must have seen it, too, because he took a step back.

"So, you think you have what it takes to take over my sister's job?" she growled.

"Well—"

"I've been looking at your records, Tinsdale. Want to know how I got access to them?" She took a step toward him. "Easy. The school *gave* them to me. They seemed to feel that *I* was a better fit for this position, so they gave *me* the records of all the monitors who would be in *my* command. They thought that *I* should review them to see who *I'd* like to cut. *Your* records were on top. They said that *I* should take a look at you first. Now, why do you think that is?"

"I—"

By now she was right up in his face. "Maybe they

think you're doing such a bang-up job that they want me to promote you. You think that's what it is?"

"I—"

"Or maybe they think you're incompetent, and the only reason you signed on to this job was so that you could hide your puny self behind that big badge of yours," she continued.

"That's not—"

"You know the funny thing, Tinsdale? A little while ago, I wasn't sure I was up for the job."

"It's true," I said. "You should have heard her."

Melanie shot me a small smirk. "But then you barged in here with your ridiculous swagger, and I thought to myself, if I don't take it, I'll be taking orders from this guy."

"You see? All you had to do was keep your mouth shut," I said.

"So, what are you saying?" he squeaked.

"I'm saying that I'm taking the job that was offered to *me*," she replied. "I guess I'm also saying that I'm your new boss—unless you feel like turning in that badge of yours."

Gerry's mouth puckered as he considered his options, none of which seemed all that appealing.

"Go ahead, Gerry," I said. "I'm sure everyone will respect you just as much without a badge."

He shot me a look, then he turned, mumbled something that sounded like "Back on patrol," and headed out the door.

"Well," I said to Melanie, "congratulations, Chief."

"Yeah. Who knew?"

"I'll be honest . . . I didn't."

"Yeah? Well, then, let's stop talking about things you don't know," she said, "and start talking about things you do. What happened to my sister?"

"I was hired by Vinny Biggs to do a drop."

"Of what?"

"Nothing illegal, or I wouldn't have done it. He's being blackmailed."

"By who?" she asked. "The Thompsons?"

"No, I don't think so. They came in like bandits, not blackmailers. Plus, the blackmailer was careful not to give any hint of his or her identity."

"So why toss that aside on the very first drop?"

"Right," I said. "Seems more likely that whoever tipped off your sister also tipped off the Thompsons. Tim and Tina had been tipped off about Melissa, and they had gotten what they'd wanted. Maybe they thought they'd find the gold at the end of the rainbow again."

"So what was your role in this?" Melanie asked.

"Vinny wanted someone who wouldn't be tempted to run off with the bag . . . someone who would just make the drop and get out of there as soon as possible."

"So, whoever's blackmailing Vinny wanted to take my sister off the board."

"Possibly. Maybe they wanted to take us both out, and I just got lucky."

"If the whole point of this was getting the bag, why lose it by hitting you two?" she asked.

"Good question. I don't know. Maybe they thought taking us out of the equation was more valuable."

Melanie turned her back to me. She sighed. "I don't know what to do."

"Most kids wouldn't," I said.

"Katie would."

I smiled. "Not necessarily. Your sister liked to haul me in here and yell at me—most of the time, I think, because she didn't know what else to do. I think it made her feel better."

"She still managed to keep things in order around here."

"Yeah. Well, except for the whole Vinny thing . . . and the Nikki hit . . . and Melissa . . . and—"

"All right, all right. I get it. She wasn't perfect." She turned to me and smiled. "Thanks, Matt. Now get the hell out of here."

"Fine," I said. "Be that way. See if I'm ever nice to you again."

"Who said you had a choice?"

16

$\mathcal{I}$ left the Kondo family office, wondering if it was possible for some good to come out of Katie's takedown. Having the chief hall monitor as an ally might come in handy. I only wished that it hadn't been at Katie's expense.

While I was thinking about this, I almost walked into Peter Kuhn. He was standing right outside the office. His eyes were bright red from crying, and his body was shaking from the consumption of at least a bag and a half of sugar, straight. He was wearing an expensive pair of jeans and an even more expensive shirt. On him, though, they looked like a new paint job on a condemned house. He didn't really pay much attention to me; he was focused on the office door that used to belong to Katie.

"You see?" he mumbled.

"Something on your mind, Pete?"

He jumped as if he hadn't noticed that I was there. Then he shook his head.

"She's gone," he croaked.

"Yeah. Something on your mind?" I asked again, this time with a little more insistence in my voice.

"She sounded like she meant it," he said, as if he had already forgotten I was standing right next to him. "She was there."

"Where, Pete? Who was where?"

His head jerked around in a series of sugar spasms. His eyes seemed to take in everything in the hallway, except my face.

"I gotta go," he mumbled.

"Wait . . . you can help with this!"

"I gotta go!" he shouted.

He started to walk away, but I grabbed him. It felt like there was an electric current running through him.

"What was in the box?" I asked.

"She's gone!"

"And you can help find who did it!" I was practically shouting. "Just tell me what was in the box!" I gave him a shake, but I don't think he noticed.

"Gone!" he yelled, as if he thought he was answering my question and it was my fault for not understanding what he meant. He twisted out of my grasp and ran away down the hall. I started to chase after him when someone stepped into my path.

"Leave him alone, Matt."

"Liz?" I was too shocked by her sudden appearance to say anything else.

"He's in bad shape, and I won't have you bullying him."

"Bullying him? Are you kidding?"

"Do I look like I'm kidding?"

"I don't know," I said. "We don't spend a lot of quality time together anymore. I've lost track of your looks."

She glared at me, then turned and started walking away.

"How do you know Pete, and why are you sticking up for him?" I asked.

She stopped but kept her back to me. "In order: I go to school here, Pete is also a student here, and although we're not friends, I know him. I'm sticking up for him because

I don't like to see anyone being bullied, especially when they're not capable of defending themselves. If I remember correctly, you used to be the same way."

"Don't try to put me on the defensive, sweetheart. You're the one walking into the middle of this play. You've got no idea what's going on, and you're trying to tell me my lines. Why are you even here?"

"I was going to see how Melanie was doing."

"You still can," I said, pointing to the door.

"My window just closed."

"Awfully narrow window."

"Are you implying something, Matt?" she asked, turning toward me. "I seem to remember you accusing me of taking out Nikki Fingers a couple of weeks ago. How'd that work out for you?"

"Well, I saved you from the Outs. Then you and I hung out in a janitor's closet. So I'd say that worked out pretty well."

She blushed, and for a moment I saw something in her face that looked like sorrow, but it was gone so fast that I might have imagined it.

"I have to go," she said.

"Liz . . ."

"What, Matt? What do you want me to tell you? That since last night I've had a change of heart? That I'm ready now to be your girlfriend?" For a moment, she sounded like she was actually saying it was so, instead of trying to prove a point. "I'm not, and I didn't. I was almost in the Outs."

"Yeah, I know," I said. "I was there."

"It changed the way I look at . . . well . . . everything."

"Since when? I mean, the past couple of weeks, you haven't even mentioned it."

"I thought I could forget about it and live a normal life," she said, "but I can't. I can't go back to being the same girl I was before."

"Who's asking you to?" I yelled. "I'm not. So why are you pushing me away?"

"Because I see what you do. You think you're fighting the system, but you're just feeding into it."

"You're kidding, right? Last night it was about other girls, and now it's about fighting the system? What are you talking about?"

"Maybe that's the problem."

"Maybe what's the problem?"

"The fact that you don't know what I'm talking about,"

she said. "Haven't you ever considered using your 'great detective skills' for something other than just making a quick buck or two . . . hiring yourself out to the highest bidder, no matter how awful they are?"

"You mean Vinny."

"How'd you guess?"

"Jeez," I said. "Wake up on the judgmental side of the bed this morning?"

"I heard you're working for him again. Didn't learn your lesson the last time? Or do you just not care?"

"Care about what?" I asked. The volume of my voice went up a few more decibels.

"About anything other than money."

"Is that what yesterday was *really* about?" I asked. "You broke up with me because all you think I care about is money?"

"All right . . . then tell me you're not working for Vinny."

"Listen, princess," I said, "I'm trying to make a little extra money so I can pay for things that my mom can't. I'm sorry if you have no idea what that's like, but that's your problem, not mine."

"Matt—"

"No. You know what? You fight your good little fight, whatever the hell it is. And then you go on back to your *big* house and your *big* restaurant that your *mommy* owns—you know, the one where your *daddy* works his employees to death and pays them as little as he legally can—and you think about all the beautiful ideals you're fighting for . . . all us lowly commoners who are too poor in either money or morals to fight your 'good fight.' Fight our battles for us, princess, because we're too stupid or corrupt to help ourselves."

Tears started to form in her eyes, but her jaw tightened in a defiant way. "You know I'm right."

"No, the only thing I know is that you shouldn't talk about things you don't have a damn clue about. Good luck with your crusade, whatever the hell it might be."

I was shaking as I walked away. The bell rang. Kids started filtering out of their classrooms and into the hall. I could hear Liz crying behind me, but I didn't turn around. "Matt," she said. "Matt, wait!"

"Yes, Matt," came a mocking voice from behind her. "Wait!"

It was Tina Thompson.

I whipped around.

Tina was holding Liz in a headlock from behind. Liz didn't look nervous—she looked pissed. Tim was standing next to her, holding a huge soaker cocked and ready. Kids in the hallway were taking notice, but they were keeping their distance.

"Careful, Matty-boy," Tina said. "You don't want to put your little girlfriend in the Outs, do you?"

Liz sighed. "Your timing really stinks."

"She's right," I said. "I was actually trying to decide if I should put her there myself."

"Shut up!" Tim yelled.

"You'd be saving me a lot of trouble," I said.

"I said, shut UP!"

"Here's how it's going to work," Tina said. "You're going to give me what you got out of that box you found, and we're going to let you go. We'll even give you back your duffel bag full of goodies. How does that sound?" She licked her lips, as if she loved the taste of her own lies.

I smiled. "Tell me what you think was in the box."

"You know what was in it," she said.

"Fine. So tell me."

She looked at me, her expression changing from cruel and triumphant to unsure and confused. "You *don't* know, do you?"

I shrugged. "Maybe I do, maybe I don't."

"Damn it!" she yelled.

"What?" Tim said, his attention now divided between me and his sister.

"They tricked us!" she yelled.

"The same person who left you that note about Melissa?" I asked. "Did they write you another note?"

Tina threw Liz on the floor and started walking away. "Do them both," she said.

As Tim pumped his soaker, a relaxed, creepy smile spread across his face. "Who's first?"

Liz backed away from him, sliding across the floor on her butt. I tensed and got ready to spring out of the way, figuring that he'd go for me first. I was still on my feet, and that made me the bigger threat.

The crowd started getting closer, but not too close. They wanted to put someone in the Outs, not become members themselves.

Tim pointed the soaker at me, then at Liz, then back at me. He looked like a kid on his birthday who couldn't decide which present to rip open first.

The soaker settled on me and lingered. His smile got a little wider. His finger closed around the trigger. My heart beat in triple time.

"Hey, Tina!" came a yell from down the hall.

All of us turned to look.

A water balloon came flying from the same direction as the voice, and it smacked Tina right in the front of her pants.

WHAP!

"AAAAAA!" Tina screamed and fell to the floor. She was about fifteen feet away from me, and my shoes still got a little wet from the blast.

Everyone in the hallway scrambled, ducking for cover. I dropped to the floor, then turned toward the direction the balloon had come from. The kid who had thrown it was already gone.

"No!" Tim's scream filled the hallway. His sister lay on the floor, the wet spot on her pants still spreading. "Nooo! Tina!"

The kids in the hallway started to come out of their hiding spots.

"Tina peed herself!" came the cry. The crowd advanced.

I didn't even try to stop them this time.

"PEE-PEE PANTS! PEE-PEE PANTS!" they chanted.

Tina was sprawled out on the floor, babbling softly to herself. Tim cradled her head in his lap. "Back! Get back!"

"PEE-PEE PANTS! PEE-PEE PANTS!" Louder and louder. Over and over again.

"Pay! You'll all pay!" he screamed, but the kids moved in anyway, laughing, pointing, and yelling.

"PEE-PEE PANTS! PEE-PEE PANTS!"

Tim waved his squirt gun around the hallway. "PAY!" The crowd took a step back but kept its shape. It didn't matter how close they stood; they didn't need to be close to send Tina to the Outs.

"PEE-PEE PANTS! PEE-PEE PANTS!"

Tim looked at his sister, wet and babbling. He looked at the squirt gun in his hand. He looked at the crowd. He smiled a weird little smile, as if a new thought had just occurred to him, a thought that suddenly put his whole life into focus. "Sister," he said. Then he turned the squirt gun toward the front of his own pants and pulled the trigger. His crotch was instantly soaked. He dropped the squirt gun, then fell to the floor next to Tina, grabbed her hand, and closed his eyes.

The crowd erupted, closing in for blood. Tim had scared them for a moment, and they were going to make him pay for it.

"FREAKS! FREAKS!"

Gerry Tinsdale must have heard the commotion because he came running around the corner like a cat hearing a can opener.

"I need backup! Now! Corridor C!" he shouted into his walkie-talkie. Then he turned on the crowd. "Hey! HEY! We're clearing this area. NOW! Suspensions to all who don't comply!"

The kids didn't move. They didn't seem to hear him over their own shouts. "FREAKS! FREAKS!"

Four more hall monitors suddenly appeared. Now everyone scattered. A couple of kids tripped over the Thompsons, who were still lying motionless on the floor.

I blended into the chaos and bolted. I looked around for Liz, to see if she was okay, but she was already gone.

$\mathcal{I}$ wandered home in a daze. My mom's car was in the driveway. Our talk wasn't until tomorrow night, but it appeared she had tonight off as well. If there was a conclusion to be drawn from this, I was in no condition to draw it.

I walked inside.

"Matt? Is everything okay?" my mom asked when she saw my face.

"Yeah. Everything's fine."

She studied me. I didn't look back at her, so as not to give anything away. I should've known it wouldn't matter.

Anyone who doesn't believe that people can read minds never really got to know their mothers.

"Come on," she said. "Put your coat back on. We're going out to eat."

"I can't. I have—" I stopped. My anger and frustration was short-circuiting my ability to conjure up a decent lie.

"Homework?" she said after a credibility-killing pause.

"Yeah."

"Well, we'll just have to get home early, then. Let's go. Chop-chop."

I opened my mouth to further my lame protest, but by that point Mom was already pushing me out the door. I sighed, then went limp and allowed myself to get caught up in her current.

A few minutes later, we were at Lucy's, our favorite sandwich shop downtown. The rest of the stores and restaurants along the river had gone upscale as the town's income bracket climbed, but Lucy's was the same hole-in-the-wall it had always been. Great food, and a lot of it, for not a lot of money.

Paulie, the tough, old ex-Navy guy behind the counter, gave us the once-over when we came in. At some point in time, everyone had decided that Paulie's general bad attitude was part of his charm. However, that just pissed him off even more. The only person in town who he didn't spit venom at was my mom.

"Hey, Kathy," he said. "What's cookin', good-lookin'?"

"Same old, same old, Paulie."

"Ain't that the truth. What'll you have?"

"Hmm." My mom always does that. She takes her time trying to decide what she's going to order, and then she always orders the same exact thing.

I was a little restless, so I blurted out, "She'll have a cheesesteak with onions and mushrooms, and I'll have the chicken Parm."

Paulie looked at me like he wasn't quite ready to acknowledge my existence, let alone take my order. Finally, he said, "I wasn't talkin' to you, kid."

"He's right, though," my mom said. "That's what I want."

Paulie nodded at her. "No problem." Then he turned to me and gave me a dirty look. "Whatsa matter, kid, huh? You in a rush? You got someplace better to be?"

Before I could answer, he turned away and started cooking. In Paulie's eyes, if you're not ordering too slowly, you're ordering too quickly.

My mom sat down at a table. I tried to sit next to her, but I was way too wound up. My foot started tapping a rhythm that any thrash metal drummer would have envied. I stood up to look out the window and started rocking back and forth on my heels.

"Is there some invisible dance contest going on that I don't know about?" my mom asked.

"Huh?"

She gave me a funny look but didn't say anything else.

"Order up!" Paulie yelled as he placed a white bag on the counter. My mom stood up and walked over to pay. "We had some extra chicken fingers, so I threw those in," he said as she handed him the money.

"Paulie . . ."

"I don't want to hear it," he said, and he gave her a look that said the discussion was over.

My mom looked at the floor, then looked back at him. Her eyes were a little watery. "Thank you."

He nodded. I thought I saw a little moisture in his eyes, too . . . but he turned away before I could confirm it.

My mom grabbed the bag, then took my arm and walked me out. The air was cool, especially after the warmth of Lucy's.

"Brrr," she said. "I'm not sure we can eat out here tonight."

"It's not that bad," I said, and it wasn't.

"I know a place we can go," she said, as if she hadn't even heard me. There was a mischievous grin on her face.

Just past the downtown area, where the number of shops shrunk down to a trickle, there was an old lighthouse. It was no longer operational, but it was still in good shape. We walked down the path that led to it. There was a small door on the side. It was locked with an ancient-looking combination lock.

"Watch out for me," my mom said, then started fiddling with the lock.

"What are you—?" I started to say, then turned my back to her and stood lookout. I tried to look casual, but it's hard to look casual when you're breaking into a lighthouse with your mom. Lucky for us, there didn't seem to be anyone else walking around.

I heard the click of the lock, and my mom opened the door, then walked inside. She ducked down a little to keep from hitting her head. "Come on," she said in a loud whisper. I followed her in.

It was pitch-black. My mom opened her cell phone.

In the dim glow, I could see metal stairs winding up to the top. She started climbing. I followed.

It was a long climb. When we got to the top, we were standing on a small platform. A ladder was bolted to one of the walls, leading up to the ceiling. My mom climbed up. When she got to the top, she put her hand on the ceiling and pushed. A trap door opened. She climbed through. Once again, I followed.

We were at the top of the lighthouse. It had been restored, but the inside still wasn't anything fancy. The people who restored it had gone for historical accuracy instead of comfort. But it was possible to see the whole city on one side and the river on the other.

"What do you think?" she asked.

"I think you're a bad example for me. Isn't this breaking and entering?"

She smiled at me. "I used to come up here all the time with your father, when we were—" She stopped. "When we just wanted to get away from the rest of the world."

"How did you find out about it?"

"Your father. He knew the family who owned it. There was only a select group of people who knew the combination to that lock downstairs, and your father was one of them."

"And he passed it to you?" I asked.

She shrugged. "Something like that."

We unwrapped our sandwiches and started eating. After a couple of bites, my mom put her sandwich down. "Feel a little better?" she asked.

"Yeah. Sorry. I was a little keyed up."

"Anything you can talk about . . . you know, before our big talk tomorrow night?"

"Why aren't we just having our talk tonight?" I asked.

She smiled. "You know when you eat the last cookie out of the bag, but you didn't know before you ate it that it was the last cookie?"

"Yeah."

"You know how you feel funky, because if you had known it was the last cookie, you would have prepared yourself a little better for it. Maybe enjoyed it a little more?"

I smiled.

"That's what tonight is," she said. "I don't know how you're going to react to what I tell you, and I have no idea how I'm going to react to what you tell me. I just wanted one more night of, well . . . this . . . before our whole relationship changes."

"You really think it will?"

"I don't know," she said. "Neither of us does."

"So, hope for the best but prepare for the worst," I said.

Mom took a huge bite of her sandwich and nodded.

"Great," I said. "I hope I didn't inherit your table manners."

She smiled with a mouth full of steak sandwich. "You see a table around here?" she asked.

"Yeah, that's exactly the kind of battle you want to win on a technicality."

"Forget everything I just said," she said. "I'm not going to miss this at all."

We ate in silence for a bit, soaking in the quiet and the beauty of the view. The sun had already gone down, but the clouds on the horizon were still backlit with a few lingering rays.

"So, I got really angry today," I said.

"What about?"

"Someone at school, someone who used to be very important to me, accused me of something."

"Something bad?"

"Not in the traditional, criminal sense," I said. "More like I was doing something for all the wrong reasons."

"Was what she said true?"

"I didn't say it was a 'she.'"

"Call it a hunch," my mom said. "Well, was it true?"

I thought about it. Did I say yes to Vinny because I wanted the money? Honestly? Of course. Someone waves forty bucks in your face, the list of reasons to say no gets shorter and much more specific.

"Maybe," I said. "But it wasn't the only reason."

"Of course not. There are very few things in life we do for only one reason. Usually, there are three or four. And some of them we'd be hard-pressed to cop to, even to ourselves."

"She made me out to be a complete jerk."

My mom shrugged. "It's a good thing she's no longer important to you."

"Yeah . . . you and I both know that's not true."

She nodded. "Listen, Matt, you have to spend years developing your moral compass, and then years more trusting that you did the right thing by following it. And you have to remember that it's *your* moral compass, not anyone else's. Others might never understand why you did what you did—and that will matter to you especially if they're the people you care about—but you have to know that you are doing the right thing for yourself. So that even if it all goes wrong, you'll know that you couldn't have made another choice."

"But what if I'm doing stuff for all the wrong reasons?"

"Really?" she asked. "*All* the wrong reasons? I doubt *all* your reasons for doing something are wrong. Maybe some are on the selfish side, but I know you. I'll tell you this, if you wait until your intentions are one hundred percent pure before you do something, you'll never do anything. You just have to believe that you're doing the right thing for mostly the right reasons. That's usually the best you can do."

"Speaking from experience?" I asked.

She smiled. "What do you think?"

"I think you should remember that speech when we talk tomorrow night."

"Hell no!" she said, then laughed. "That speech applies to you and other people, not me. I'm your mother, so I have the right to be as irrational as I want."

"That hardly seems fair."

"Sorry, kid. Them's the rules."

"One more question," I said.

"Shoot."

"Can we stay up here for a while longer?"

She leaned over and gave me a kiss on the forehead. "As long as you'd like."

We sat and ate the rest of our sandwiches as the lights from the city turned the water into a sparkling gown.

I woke up the next morning at 6:15. I was still tired but feeling better than I had a right to. If I managed to get through the day without landing in the Outs, I'd get to come home and find out just how messed up my family life really was. Oh, and I'd also get to tell Mom about all the stuff that went on at school, which probably meant that she was going to blow the whistle on everyone, practically guaranteeing me a spot in the Outs.

And yet, despite all of this, I felt pretty good. Maybe last night with my mom, even though it might be the last of its kind, was what I needed to gain a little clarity.

When I walked into the kitchen, there was a note on the counter. "See you tonight. Can't wait to tell my story! (Sarcasm, in case ya didn't know . . .) Love ya, Mom." I made a cup of hot cocoa to try to wake myself up a little, then went down to my office.

I looked at the copy of the blackmailer's note Vinny had given to me and compared it with the piece of paper I found in the box, the one with the letter/number series that matched the one the police had found in my father's car. Just from the samples in front of me, the handwriting looked completely different. Not that that meant anything. The handwriting on the letter looked like the writer had tried to disguise his or her real handwriting. It was sloppy—in a calculated way. By comparison, the letters and numbers on the slip of paper were written neatly, as if that writer wanted to make sure no one misread any of the characters.

I picked up the box with the carved top. I checked the inside for the seventy-fifth time; it was still empty. I put it down. It had no more secrets to tell.

I wasn't sure what to do next, so I pulled last year's yearbook out from a stack of books near my desk, hoping for a little bit of historical context. I flipped through it until I found the cheerleader page. I looked at the girls' faces, bright and happy. There was Gretchen, her grin hinting at the malevolence that would later prove her undoing. There was Melissa, her expression bright and innocent, as if she didn't know how to play the game yet and was just happy to be there.

And then there was Cynthia. She was pretty in this picture—really pretty—but her beauty was more subdued, not as fierce as I knew it. Something inside of me skipped to a weird rhythm just thinking about her. Cynthia was the girl who defied all my expectations; the girl who made me think of cheerleaders as something more than just mindless robots concerned about their status and not other people's feelings.

I looked at Melissa again. She hadn't been dating Will at the time of the photo. She was just another sixth grader, happy to have made the squad, to have found a place where she belonged, where she was accepted. She had slipped into an identity early and knew exactly where it was going to take her over the next three years, and possibly beyond. She had no idea how wrong she was.

I stood up, still looking at the black-and-white pixels that constituted Melissa's face. Her perfect hair was now in straggly ruins. The eyes that had been bright with excitement were now dulled with dread. Her spirit, her soul, had been snuffed out, and I was not about to let that go unpunished. I folded over the top corner of the page, then closed the yearbook and shoved it in my bag. I wanted to be able to remind myself of what was at stake.

Before I left, I picked up the two pieces of paper on my desk, the ones that had my dad's clue written on them. I put the original back in my desk drawer, where it belonged. I put the other one in my back pocket.

When I got to school, the steps were filled with kids staying outside as long as possible in order to delay the inevitable.

Going from the cold outside to the heated inside always made me feel weird, as if someone had spritzed my face with water, then held a heater directly on it. I peeled off my jacket and threw it in my locker. I almost didn't see the cell phone sitting on my shelf.

It was nothing too fancy; the kind they give you when you open up a new account or that a parent hands down to a kid. I handled it gently, as if it was made of paper and my hands were wet. I almost dropped it when it rang.

I waited for the third ring before I answered. "Hello?"

"Matt?" a voice whispered.

"Speaking. Who's this?"

"I'd rather not say right now."

"Can you speak up?" I asked. "I can hardly hear you."

"If you can't hear me," the voice whispered, "I might as well hang up."

"Fine," I said. "We'll play it your way. What do you want?"

"I want you to look at something for me, but I don't want to show it to you."

"O-kayyy . . . Is this a riddle? Because I hate riddles."

"I know better. You didn't think I gave you a phone just to talk to you, did you?"

"I have no idea why you gave me a phone."

"You do now." There was a click as the whisperer hung up. I looked at the display. There was only one bar of battery life left. Whatever was on this phone, I had to find it in a hurry.

The first thing I checked was the contacts list. It was empty. I checked messages (voice and text), recent call records, mobile e-mail accounts. Nothing. Then I checked pictures. There was one. The battery life bar was blinking. I had very little time left. I selected the photo so that it filled the phone's screen, but the picture was still too small to make out any details. All I could see was that there were two figures facing each other, as if they were talking or shaking hands.

I turned the phone off. There was no sense staring at the picture. It wasn't getting any clearer, and all I was doing was wasting what little battery life was left. I needed help, and at the moment, there was only one kid I trusted with something like this.

I had seven minutes before I had to get to homeroom. I had to hustle if I was going to catch him in his office. I closed my locker door, then turned to run. Standing in front of me was Jenny Finnegan.

"Pardon me," I said.

She stood there and smirked at me.

"All right, let's try this, then," I said. "Get the hell out of my way."

"Vinny wants to talk to you."

I laughed. "Is this your new job? Vinny's message girl? Refresh my memory, did Nikki ever have to do anything like this?"

Her face tightened. "I can't wait to see how smug you are when I put you in the Outs."

"You? Put me in the Outs? Ha! I've seen you work

under pressure, sweetheart. All I need to do is say 'Boo!' and I've got you on the run."

Her hands ducked behind her and came back out with two squirt guns . . . little pink numbers. I had to admit, she was pretty fast.

"What do you have to say now, Matt? Huh? Something smart, I'm sure."

I laughed. "Who are you trying to fool? I hope it isn't me. If Vinny wanted me in the Outs, he wouldn't send you."

"I'll say it was an accident."

"I hope one of his operatives heard that. I want Vinny to hear how stupid you think he is, that he'd fall for a lie that bad."

"There aren't any operatives, sweetie. Just me and you."

"Oh yeah? Tell that to Ricky Ryan over there," I said, pointing behind me. "He's in Vinny's crew, right? Because he's been watching us like we're a Vegas floor show and his girlfriend's in the chorus."

Jenny was rattled. She tried to hide it, but she wasn't good at improvisation.

"Or Susan Myers," I continued. "She must be really

thirsty. She's been drinking from that water fountain for the past five minutes."

Jenny looked over at Susan, slowly, as if she didn't want to but had run out of the willpower to stop herself. Susan looked back at her and winked. A brief window opened, so I jumped through it. I grabbed both squirt guns and ripped them out of her hands. I threw them behind me. They clattered down the hall. One of them cracked. Water started puddling around it.

"You want to be tough?" I asked. "You should probably be a little more focused."

Jenny looked like she was about to jump on me and rip my throat out with her teeth. Something behind me caught her eye. I turned to see Ricky Ryan leveling his gaze at her. His head was moving gently from side to side. Jenny backed down, but only physically. Her expression was still full of the painful possibilities she was conjuring up for me.

"If that's all," I said, "I have someplace to be."

She didn't say anything. Just stared at me. Ricky Ryan was still doing his headshake, but this time it seemed to be indicating a direction. He was telling Jenny to follow him.

She pushed past me, then turned and walked backward

down the hallway. She picked up the squirt gun that lay unbroken on the ground, all the while not taking her eyes off me. When she was close, Ricky took her by the arm and guided her away.

Susan Myers approached me. "Vinny wants to talk to you."

"Yeah, I heard. I've got someplace to be right now."

She pulled a squirt gun on me, but her heart wasn't in it.

"Yeah, that's not going to work," I said. "You need me for something or you would've let little Miss Jenny pop me just now. She blew the bluff and trashed your leverage."

Susan sighed and put her squirt gun away. Then she whistled, and the two hulking eighth graders who grabbed me on Monday appeared out of nowhere. "She didn't trash all of my leverage."

"Touché," I said. "If it's all the same to you, I'd rather walk than be carried."

"Follow me," she said, and flashed me what appeared to be a genuine smile. She glanced at Jenny, who was a few paces ahead of us, then looked back at me and rolled her eyes. "Amateur," she said.

I grinned. Jenny might never get all the comeuppance

she deserved—at least not in any obvious way—but it looked like she hadn't gained anyone's respect. She wasn't about to make people forget about her sister.

We walked over to a janitor's closet. Jenny was standing like a sentinel outside, trying not to make eye contact with me. It was obvious that Ricky had had a little talk with her. Susan motioned for me to go in. I nodded to her. "You better keep an eye on that one," I said, pointing to Jenny. "She's 'dangerous.'"

Susan and Ricky both snickered. I was pretty sure I could hear Jenny's teeth grinding.

I walked into the closet. Vinny was sitting in a chair, surrounded by the same enormous goons as before.

"You're doing a great job with Jenny," I said. "It only took two more of your 'employees' to help her do a simple job correctly."

One of Vinny's guards stepped forward and sucker punched me in the gut. I felt like I was going to throw up my last four meals. I staggered backward, until my back hit the door.

"That's for being a hypocrite," Vinny said. "*You* had the simple job of dropping off a duffel bag in a locker, and you managed to screw that up."

"Yeah, like it wasn't the blackmailer who tipped off Katie and the Thompsons," I said sarcastically. "You'd have to be stupid to think that first drop-off was anything other than a setup, and I know you're not stupid. So I have to think you were just looking for an excuse to have me punched in the stomach."

"I don't need an excuse."

"You do now. The next kid that tries gets his hand broken."

"You still have a job to do."

"The hell I do."

"You botched up the first time, so now you get to do it again," he said.

A tall, thin kid standing behind Vinny held an envelope out to me. I glared at Vinny. "Take the envelope, Matthew," he said.

"I don't take orders from—"

"Take it!" he yelled. "Take it or I'll have them staple it to your chest."

Five of the goons moved toward me in unison. I grabbed the envelope out of the skinny kid's hand. There was another ransom note inside. It was a photocopy. I skimmed it. Another drop. 6:55 tomorrow morning. Same place: locker 416. I put the note back in the envelope.

"Okay," I said, "so now the only thing left between us, Vinny, is for you to tell me what was in the photo."

Vinny flinched. I had surprised him. "None of your business," he said, recovering quickly.

"Sure it is. You made it my business. Now tell me."

He stood up. His hands tightened into fists. "*You* don't give *me* orders!"

"Tell me."

He punched me in the face. It wasn't the hardest punch I'd ever gotten, but I'd never mistake it for a kiss on the cheek. His guards took a step closer to us, but they looked unsure about what to do.

"Wow," I said, rubbing my jaw. "Those gym classes are really paying off for you. Feel better now?"

Vinny was breathing hard and massaging the knuckles on his hand. He looked confused, as if he was unsure of where he was and why his knuckles hurt.

"What happened to you?" I asked.

"You know what happened to me," he said. "You know why I do this."

"You don't have to anymore. You've proved your point."

His eyes were set and stony.

"But it's not really about that anymore, is it?" I asked.

"It's something different now. The bullied has become the bully."

Vinny glared at me. "This is it, Matthew . . . your last case," he said. "I bet you didn't think this day would come, but I assure you, it's here."

"You're a fortune-teller now?"

"I'm not telling your future," he said, "I'm making it." Vinny looked at the skinny kid behind him. The kid grabbed a duffel bag and handed it to me.

"You screwed up," Vinny said, "and I can't let a thing like that go unpunished. Plus, quite frankly, I'm sick of you . . . you and your smug, superior attitude."

"Look who's talking," I said.

"I think it's time you had a view of the Outs from the inside, Matthew. Maybe you'll learn that you should've been taking it seriously all along. So, do the job right this time and you'll only get splashed."

"Your pep talks need a little work," I said.

"Do it wrong or don't do it at all, and . . . well, you remember Triple D?"

I did. Triple D stood for Dirty Diaper Dexter, one of the first kids Vinny ever put in the Outs. The whole school had found Triple D slumped over one of the bike racks, wearing nothing but a diaper, the front of which was soaked with yellow liquid; the back was smeared with . . . well, use your imagination. I heard through a reliable source that it was actually chocolate, but no one cared enough to set the record straight. He was so far in the Outs, he was the guy other kids in the Outs knocked around when *they* wanted someone to bully.

"Go ahead, Matthew," Vinny snarled. "Say something smart."

I opened the bag. It was the same as before: four boxes of candy and a large stack of cash. I smiled. "I don't have to, do I? The smell of flop sweat speaks for itself."

I opened the door and walked out. No one followed me. Susan was still standing outside the door, but Ricky and Jenny were gone. "How'd it go?" she asked, as if I was coming from somewhere normal, like taking a quiz.

"Not bad. Could've been worse."

"Still might be."

"Sure . . . but I doubt it. Might want to get your résumé together," I said. "I have a feeling you'll be looking for work soon."

"I've already got a couple of things lined up," she said, "but thanks for the advice." I gave her a puzzled look, but all she did was smile at me. "See you around, Stevens." She turned away. As far as she was concerned, our conversation was over.

It was a long walk back to my locker to grab my first-period books. I was a little shaky. I had never seen Vinny that panicky before. The good news was that he was distracted, which might make him sloppy. The bad news was that he seemed determined to put me in the Outs, and sloppy or not, he had the means to get it done. I had one day to find some wiggle room. And I still had to talk to Jimmy Mac.

The rest of my morning was filled with classes I couldn't get out of. As soon as the lunch bell rang, I went to the cafeteria to grab lunch before heading over to Jimmy's office. I was halfway through my hot dog when I spotted Nicole Finnegan, a.k.a. the former Nikki Fingers, sitting at a table by herself, mumbling into her sandwich. Someone was walking toward her. It was Katie Kondo. She may have been in the Outs, too, but you wouldn't know it by looking at her. She looked the same, dressed the same, had the same almost-a-scowl expression on her face. The

Outs was like an invisible symbol hanging over her head. Every kid in school knew it was there, but Katie would be damned if she would give in to it. She stood across from Nicole and asked her a question.

Nicole looked up slowly, as if she were expecting someone to hit her with a pie. When she saw Katie, her expression changed from fear to confusion. There was Katie Kondo, former chief of the hall monitors, former scourge of the underworld, the girl who would not rest until she brought Nikki down, asking Nicole for permission to sit across from her. Nicole nodded yes.

Katie sat down. Her facial expression wasn't exactly friendly, but it wasn't hostile, either. There was a look that I had never seen on her face before: empathy. They ate in silence, but something changed in Nicole, almost instantaneously. She still looked disheveled . . . but now she looked a little less disoriented, as if Katie's presence had made her a little less crazy somehow. Her whole body seemed to relax.

Randy Sloan, one of the least-funny class clowns in history, approached their table. He made some remark that I couldn't hear, but I knew it wasn't funny. Of course, Randy started laughing hysterically. The two tables nearby started laughing, too. Randy beamed like the gap-toothed idiot that he was. One problem: Katie and Nicole didn't react.

It wasn't that they didn't notice him. They both turned their heads to look at him, their expressions blank and bland, as if Randy had just told them that the temperature in the cafeteria was a comfortable 71 degrees. This was not the reaction that Randy was expecting, and it ticked him off. "Skanks!" he shouted.

Katie looked at Nicole and rolled her eyes. Nicole smirked back. It was tiny, and if I hadn't been standing there studying them, I might have missed it. It made me think about the precariously balanced set of conditions that made the Outs effective, and wonder what would happen if those conditions started to tip toward one end.

I stopped wondering when Randy grabbed Katie's lunch, threw it on the floor, and stepped on it. Actually, he didn't just step on it; he ground it into the floor. Then he reached over and gave her a condescending pat on the cheek. I was out of my seat and moving.

Before Randy could pull his hand away, Katie grabbed his wrist. In a half-heartbeat, almost every kid in the lunch room stood up and fixed a cold stare at Katie. They were united in making sure that someone in the Outs didn't forget their place.

Katie's eyes went wide. She hadn't expected this, but she was too pigheaded to back down. Randy was sneering at her. He was about to say something mean when I buried my shoulder into his stomach. "Guuuuf!" he said, as I knocked the air out of his lungs. Of all the things Randy's ever said, "Guuuuf!" was the closest to actually being funny.

He landed on the floor with another "Guuuuf!" I was really starting to like that sound.

Katie leaned toward me. "I could've handled it," she said quietly.

"Shut up and sit down," I said, just as quietly. "Slowly. Now's not the time to make a stand."

She looked around the cafeteria. Every kids' eyes were on her. She sat down, but didn't look happy about it. Everyone else in the caf sat down, too. After a moment they went back to their business, as if they had never been interrupted.

"You owe me," I said, "and here's how I want to get paid. It may not happen today, or tomorrow, or the day after that, but one day soon, I want you two to remind yourselves who you were before you were put in the Outs. And if you can't remind yourselves, remind each other. The revolution starts with the two of you."

Nicole and Katie looked up at me, and for a moment I saw the girls as they were just a few short weeks ago: the brains, the ferocity. Their sly grins told me all I needed to know. I grinned back at them, then checked the clock on the wall. Ten minutes left to talk to Jimmy Mac. I gave them both a quick and casual salute, then headed for the exit.

Jimmy Mac's office was a small room off the gym that used to be a supply closet. There were piles of newspapers everywhere. It felt like it would be a fire hazard to just say the word "match."

Jimmy didn't seem pleased to see me. "What do you want?" he said.

"I need your help with something."

"I'm busy."

"This is important."

"And what? What I do isn't important?"

"I didn't mean it like that."

"Yes, you did," he said. "You're Mr. Important Matt

Stevens. Mr. Big Shot. So, am I supposed to be honored that you need my help?"

"What's gotten into you?"

"What do you mean? Just because I'm not falling all over myself to do your job for you?"

My first instinct was to grab him and slam him into one of his piles of paper. But this was Mac, the one kid in school I trusted. I took a deep breath, and told my temper to take a hike.

"This is about Cynthia," I asked, "isn't it?"

He was itching for a fight, but my change in tone took the wind out of his sails. He hid his face from me. I heard a definite sniffle.

"You had to take her, didn't you?" he asked.

"I didn't 'take' anyone, Mac, and you know it. I can't control Cynthia any more than you can."

He sighed and looked at the floor. "I know, Matt. I know. It's just—" He looked at me as if he wanted me to finish his sentence for him. When I didn't, he continued. "It's just that I've had a thing for her forever . . . I mean, who wouldn't? And then you swoop in. How'm I supposed to compete with you?"

"Compete with me? Mac, I'm a mess."

"Yeah, well, Cynthia doesn't think so."

"I didn't lead her on, really. In fact, I told her I wasn't interested."

"It doesn't matter. She wants you. You've got everything she's looking for," he said, "and I'm just some pathetic little kid, too weak to be of any use to her."

"That's a load of crap," I said. "Listen, Mac, you're the only kid in this godforsaken place that I'd trust with my life."

He looked surprised and pleased, in spite of himself. "You mean that?"

"No. In fact, on the way over here, I told six other kids the exact same thing," I said sarcastically. "Yes, of course I mean it!"

"You know what? Look . . . forget it, okay? You got something you need help with, and I'm jawing on and on about my love life," he said.

I didn't say anything.

"Come on," he said. "Seriously, I feel like a fool already."

I nodded, but made a mental note to revisit this topic. I liked Jimmy a lot, and I didn't want something like this to come between us. I held out the cell phone that was put in my locker. "There's one photo on this. I need you to enlarge it."

He took the phone out of my hand. "Yeah, okay."

"It doesn't have a lot of juice left," I said, "and I don't have the charger, so you'll have to work quickly."

"Got it. Anything I should be looking for?"

"From what I understand, whatever's in that photo is going to be hard to miss. But it needs to be enlarged. The screen on the phone is too small."

His eyes lit up with the fire I was so familiar with. "How big we talking here?"

"The picture or the story?" I asked.

"Both."

"First, I think you better get a heavier lock for that door," I said, and pointed toward the entrance of his office.

"That big?" He smiled.

"I think so, yeah. How large can you make the picture and still have it look clear?" I asked.

He thought about it for a second. "I had a story last year about some kid skimming money off his holiday wrapping paper sales. The evidence was a photo of something else—two little kids playing in the park, I think. The kid skimming money was a tiny image in the left corner of the picture. When we blew that sucker up, it was clear as day."

"Can I see it?"

"Sure, yeah! Hold on . . . " He pulled out a large book and started skimming through it. "Here it is . . . *The Franklin Gazette*, issue twenty-eight, page one. March of last year."

I suddenly felt dizzy. My vision blurred. A moment of inspiration was hitting me square between the eyes.

"You okay, Matt?"

"Yeah . . ." I shook my head and tried to regain my composure. "Yeah, I'm okay. Say that again."

"Say what again?"

"Wait, hold on . . . do you have a pen?"

"Yeah. Here."

I took the pen, then reached into my back pocket and pulled out the little piece of paper. "Now, say that again."

"What?"

"The issue . . . of the newspaper . . . that the photo was in."

"Ohhhh! One of the March issues, the date was—"

"No, not the date. Say it like you said it before. Exactly like you said it before."

I must've looked pretty crazed, because Jimmy gave me a look. I couldn't tell if he was scared *for* me, or *of* me.

"*The Franklin Gazette*, issue twenty-eight, page one."

As he spoke, I wrote it down.

"Are you sure you're okay?" he asked.

"Yeah," I said. "Does this look right to you?" I showed him the piece of paper that I'd just written on. At the top was my father's clue: TMS136P15. Right below it was what Jimmy Mac had just told me: TFG28P1.

"Yeah," he said, but he looked confused. "What's that top one?"

I took a deep breath. My hand was shaking. "I think I'm about to find out."

The public library was pretty empty at that time of day. Just a few older people sitting in the quiet room across from the main desk, reading newspapers, and a couple of moms with toddlers in the children's room. The man behind the desk eyed me suspiciously. "Shouldn't you be in school?" he asked.

"School project," I said, putting on the most innocent face I could manage under the circumstances.

He studied me for a moment, but he looked more amused than annoyed. "If you say so," he said.

I put the piece of paper on the desk and tapped it. "TMS," I said. "Is there a newspaper or magazine that has a title—"

"With words beginning with the letters *T*, *M*, and *S*?" he asked. "Let's find out. Follow me."

He walked out from behind the desk and headed for a doorway to the right, into a large room with about twelve rows of metal racks. Each rack was full of cardboard boxes, stacked high; each of the boxes was filled with newspapers.

"We're trying to scan all these into the computer so we can get rid of the hard copies, but it's slow work," he said. We walked over to a table against the wall. There was a computer there that looked almost as old as me. He sat down in front of it. "Let me see that thing again."

I showed it to him.

"So, where do you think we should start?" he asked.

I looked at the clue, and at Jimmy Mac's version below it. "I think we should look for something small and local," I said, not sure where my theory was coming from but feeling it was true somehow. "I feel like something big like *The New York Times* or *The Boston Globe* wouldn't be classified by issue number; it would be referred to by date."

The librarian nodded. "Makes sense."

"The newspaper in town is called *The Daily Review*," I said, thinking out loud.

"And of the other ones nearby, none of them have the initials *TMS* in the title."

"That means it could be a local newspaper from anywhere," I said. My hopes of this being easy were quickly evaporating. "Was *The Daily Review* ever called anything else? Was there another newspaper that used to—"

The expression on the librarian's face made me stop. He looked as if a bolt of lightning had struck him in the head. "There was a small local paper that my mom used to pick up at the grocery store," he said. "It's not like she'd make a special trip to get it or anything. It was just, if we were out and she saw it and remembered to pick it up, she would. It had a lot of ads from local businesses in it."

"What was it called?"

"*The Merchant Saler*, spelled *s-a-l-e-r*. Not a bad pun, actually."

My hands started shaking. "Did you scan those into the computer?"

"No. But I do think we have a couple of boxes of them around here somewhere." He stood up and started walking through the aisles. He pulled a box out but, after a quick look, put it back. He did that a couple more times before he hit pay dirt. "Here they are."

My heart was pounding as he handed me the box.

"I think there's another box around here, too," he said, then started walking through the aisles again.

I sat on the floor and carefully pulled all the newspapers out of the box. They smelled old and musty, like my basement office; it gave me a strange feeling, almost like déjà vu. I flipped through them. They weren't in any kind of order. Issue 213 was on top of issue 34, which was on top of issue 114. The chances of finding issue 136 in this box were slim.

"I've found some more," the librarian called out from across the room.

I smiled, then picked up the last five in my box. Issue 136 was two up from the bottom.

I looked at the issue number again, sure that I had seen it wrong, that maybe it said *36*. I blinked, rubbed my eyes, and stared at it again. It still said *issue 136*.

The librarian came walking over with the other box. "You found it," he said.

"I did."

• • •

Back out in the main room, I sat and stared at the newspaper lying on the table in front of me. I couldn't bring myself to open it yet. I was almost afraid to touch it.

I glanced up at the front desk. The librarian was back at work, but he was keeping an eye on me. He seemed genuinely concerned; I gave him a little smile to try to let him know I was okay. I guess it wasn't my best smile, because it made him look even more concerned.

I looked down at the newspaper. I closed my eyes and took a deep breath . . . and placed my left hand flat on the newspaper. My thumb felt for the lower-right corner. I took another deep breath and opened my eyes. I turned the page, and didn't stop until I had hit page 15.

The two photocopies were folded up and tucked into the back pocket of my jeans.

The sooner I could get them into the filing cabinet in the basement, the better I'd feel. So, I walked faster.

When I got home, my mom's car wasn't in the driveway. I knew she wasn't working at the restaurant, because we were going to have our talk later that night.

Our talk. The photocopies. In my back pocket.

I ran around back, to the door to my basement office.

Jimmy Mac was leaning against the door, his head moving around erratically, as if he was expecting an ambush.

"Mac. You all right?"

"What happened to you today?" he asked. "You disappeared."

"I had something I needed to do. Are you okay?"

"I've got something to show you." He held up the manila envelope and gave it a little shake. "Inside."

"Of course."

I opened the door. He followed me in, closing the door behind him.

I sat down at my desk; he sat in the chair across from me. Before I could say anything, he threw the envelope on the table. It slid over to me. I stopped it with my hand.

"An eight-by-ten glossy, lightened up to show some faces," he said. "They're some interesting faces."

I opened the envelope and pulled the picture out. The faces were interesting, all right. My mind was racing, making all the connections that were obvious now that the circuit had been closed. "Did anyone see you with this?"

"My mom, but I'm pretty sure she's on my side."

I looked at the photo again, then quickly put it back in the envelope. "With something like this, I'm not sure I'd even trust *her*."

I heard the latch to the door click softly. I jumped up. Jimmy didn't move.

"What are you guys talking about?" Cynthia asked as she walked in.

"What are you doing here?" I asked, taken completely off-guard.

"The door was unlocked."

I shot a look at Jimmy, but his eyes were directed at the floor. I smelled a setup.

"What are you guys talking about?" she asked again.

"Nothing," I said.

"Sure looked like something."

"Well, that just means your imagination is better than your eyesight," I said.

"What's in the envelope?" she asked.

"None of your business," I answered.

"I hired you. Consequently, it is my business."

"Cute little logic problem you've got figured out, there," I said. "Unfortunately, I didn't take my smart pills this morning, so I'm just going to go with 'Nuh-uh.'"

"Just show her the photo, Matt," Jimmy said.

I shot him an angry look.

"You guys are really cute, you know that?" I said. "Why go through all this, though? You charmed Mac to get in here . . . why didn't you just charm him into showing you the photo?"

"He wouldn't."

"Not mine to show," Jimmy said.

"So just show me, Matt. Or Jimmy's going to tell me. I know a picture is worth a thousand words, but I'm pretty sure that he can boil it down to a sentence or two."

"He wasn't going to show you, but now he'll tell you?"

"I didn't think you'd be so stubborn about it," Mac said.

"He actually respects me," she said.

"Yeah, well, I don't think Jimmy's thinking straight," I said. "I think that if he was, he'd realize that telling you what's in the photo would be putting you in the line of fire."

"Or maybe Jimmy's not a male chauvinist and respects me enough to realize that I can take care of myself."

"You know how I can tell that someone can't take care of themselves?" I said. "They usually say something brilliant like 'I can take care of myself,' and actually believe it."

"How condescending of you," she said, then turned to Jimmy. "Tell me what's in the photo."

"Don't tell her," I said.

"Tell me!"

"Shut up! Both of you!" Jimmy shouted, loud enough to make me hope my mom wasn't upstairs. "I'm sick of both of you. I just want to go home. You work this out. You don't need me." He got up to leave. I got up with him, but Cynthia stepped right in my path. Jimmy saw this. His frown sunk even deeper as he walked out the door.

"He likes you. A lot. And he thinks that you like me instead."

"He's right. Now show me the picture."

I choked, then coughed, even though there was nothing in my mouth but saliva.

"You think it's an accident that he's a damn good reporter?" she asked. "He's got instincts, and eyes . . . something that you don't seem to have, which makes me wonder what kind of detective you are."

"You're going to have to do a lot more than tell me you like me to get me to show you—"

She cut me off with a kiss. It was long and slow. I tasted peppermint, like she had just licked a candy cane. My head was buzzing when she pulled away.

"Does that qualify as 'a lot more'?" she asked.

"Maybe," I said, trying to sound jaded and unaffected, but that's hard to do when you're floating six inches off the ground.

"Silly, Matthew," she said, then came in close again. "Keep the photo to yourself . . . just kiss me again."

"No. Maybe I'm a hopeless romantic, but I like to kiss girls who aren't trying to seduce something out of me."

She pulled back from me. She didn't pout. It wasn't in her nature. "I'm impressed and amazed by how stupid you are," she said with a smile.

"Most people are."

"All right . . . hold on to your photo. Just tell me what's happening so I can help you."

"If you want to help me, go home."

"Listen, Matt, you can't stop me from helping you. We're locked in the same building for seven hours a day."

"Yeah, I know. Just give me a day to see this through, my way . . . on my own."

"What is it with you? I'd chalk it up to male macho crap, but you don't seem the type."

"I'm not. You know how many girls have knocked me around? The only way I could still be a male chauvinist is if I had frequent memory loss."

"Then what is it?"

I took a couple of steps away from her and thought of the photocopies that were still in my back pocket. "There's an aspect of this case that no one else knows about. It's personal."

She stared at me. "Oh," she said. Her face fell. "It's something to do with Liz, isn't it?"

I didn't contradict her.

"Okay," she said quietly. She turned away from me. "I guess that makes me an idiot."

"No. I'm pretty sure that makes me an idiot. And I can think of a hundred boys who would back me up on that."

She didn't say anything. She just stood there with her back to me. It took all of my willpower to not put my hand on her shoulder . . . turn her around . . . and kiss her.

"I just want to get through this case first," I continued. "Get my head straight. And I can't do that when you're around me."

"Don't do that," she said.

"Do what?"

"Give me hope."

"I'm not trying to," I said. "I'm just trying to be honest."

"Finish the case," she said. "Your own way. And hurry up about it. I want you thinking straight when I kiss you again."

"All right," I said. "The drop is at seven tomorrow morning. After that, one way or another, I should be finished. You might want to wait until then before you commit to kissing me."

She touched my cheek. "I'll see you tomorrow."

I didn't exhale until she was gone.

I went back to my desk and pulled the photocopies I got from the library out of my back pocket but didn't look at them. I needed to stay logical . . . unemotional . . . and looking at those photocopies didn't allow for that.

I took the newest blackmail note that I'd gotten from Vinny out of my front pocket. I studied it again, looking for anything that might narrow down the field a bit. There was nothing in the content, but on the bottom there were a few markings that I hadn't noticed before. They looked like pen taps, indentations that wouldn't necessarily show up on the original but showed up on the photocopy. I went into my desk drawer and took out the first blackmail note. The marks were at the bottom of that one, too. I read both notes again, and other things popped out at me, clues that seemed obvious now.

I had a phone book on my desk. I flipped through it until I found the number I was looking for. I picked up the phone and dialed.

The kid picked up on the second ring.

"Hello?"

"I have something you're going to want to see," I said. I slid one of the photos out of the manila envelope, looked at it, then slid it back in.

"Matt?"

"Yeah," I said. "Tomorrow morning. Seven A.M. Locker 416. And bring some money. You lied to me, and now you're going to pay for it."

I hung up. I sat and looked at the outside of the envelope. I didn't want to look at the pictures again. I wanted to take my mind off what tomorrow was going to be like, but the only thing I had to distract me was thinking about my talk with my mom.

I rested my head on my desk and drifted into a

troubled sleep. I dreamt I was on the basketball team and I was trying to dribble the ball, but it wouldn't bounce back up to me. It just sat deflated on the floor. Everyone I knew was in the stands; they were all booing me. Someone walked out of the gym in disgust. I didn't see who it was, but I knew it was my dad.

21

I woke up a short time later. I wiped my face with my hands a couple of times and checked the clock: 5:07 P.M.

I opened my desk drawer. I picked up all the notes and photocopies—anything having to do with the case— and placed them on the desktop. I put them in order, chronologically—not when they happened but the timing with which I thought they pertained to the case. I told myself the story of how I thought it had all gone down.

I checked the clock again: 5:30.

I picked up one of the photocopies I got from the

library and walked upstairs. It was time to find out what it meant to my mom.

She was in the kitchen drying the dishes. There was a mug of coffee on the counter that she was taking occasional sips from. She was working but obviously distracted, as she didn't hear me come in until the door closed behind me.

She jumped a little, almost dropping her mug. A little bit of coffee slopped onto her hand. "Jeez! Matt!" She was smiling, but she was nervous . . . jumpy. "Sneaking up on me?"

"In a way," I said.

She gave me a funny look.

"There's a kid in my school named Vincent Biggio, but everyone calls him Vinny Biggs," I said. "He used to be the target of bullies, but now he runs a whole criminal organization."

"Matt, what are you—"

"Vinny controls just about everything that happens in school, illegal or otherwise," I continued. "None of it is too bad . . . well, except for the test-stealing and the gambling ring."

"Gambling?"

"But worse than that, he humiliates kids and ruins their lives. He started doing it last year as a way to get back at some of the bullies who had wronged him. And since he was focusing on jerks and bullies, giving them a taste of their own medicine, everyone went along with it. Then things started getting out of control. Vinny began using it as a punishment for anyone who crossed him, even in little ways. Kids who hadn't done anything to anyone suddenly found themselves in the Outs."

"The Outs?" she asked.

"That's the club you end up in if you get marked," I answered.

"Marked?"

"Vinny has his assassins mark the victims by squirting them with liquid in the front of their pants. The victim is then called 'Pee-Pee Pants' and—hey!—welcome to the Outs! That kid's social status is ruined for as long as he stays in this town . . . and in more than a few cases, even if he manages to leave."

She looked confused, as if she wasn't sure whether she should be concerned or amused. "Pee-Pee Pants? Seriously?" she asked. "Don't you think it's a little—"

"Childish? Yup, which is exactly why he chose that

method. Vinny knew what he was doing. He knew that he couldn't keep his operation a secret from adults forever. So he picked a method of humiliation that most grown-ups would look at and say, 'Well, that's childish. They'll grow out of that soon. And no one's *really* getting hurt.'"

"So kids just laugh and yell 'pee-pee' at each other?" she asked.

"Well, that's one way to look at it. Another way to look at it is that kids single out other kids to completely humiliate and destroy. Whether they yell 'pee-pee pants' or 'bologna breath' or 'big nose' or 'lard butt' doesn't matter, the end result is the same."

"So, what's your role in all this?"

"Kids hire me to help them through their problems," I said.

She nodded. "Like a private detective."

I nodded.

"And you're in trouble?"

"Always. Not with my teachers or the principal or anything," I said. "More like with the kids who do stuff and don't want to get caught."

"So, I should stop this, right? I mean, I can't let this continue."

"Yeah, well, you kind of have to. Vinny's already prepared for that scenario. You'll stop the whole squirt-gun thing, but then he'll just pick some other form of humiliation. It won't stop. And for me, things will get a whole lot worse."

"What should I do, then?"

"No idea," I said. "Vinny is smart, and he understands the system. He doesn't leave any evidence that could be connected back to him, so even if you'd convince the school administration that this is all going on under their noses, you might be able to take out a few of Vinny's foot soldiers, but there's no way you can stick him with the blame."

She scrunched up her face. "Well, this is frustrating."

"Yeah, I know. But I guarantee you, if you try to blow the whistle on him, I'll be beaten . . . relentlessly . . . for as long as we live here."

"So I just have to sit here and watch this happen?"

I nodded. "But there is one thing you can do for me."

"Anything."

"Things are going to change for me tomorrow, and not for the better."

"Matt—"

"It's okay. I've made my peace with it. In fact, in some ways it might actually be a good thing."

"In what way?"

"It can't go on like this forever. I'm sick to death of it. Too many kids I know—good kids—have gotten hurt," I said. "I didn't realize it until the other day, but there's a delicate balance to the Outs, and it may be reaching its tipping point."

"And you think you might be the difference?"

I shrugged. "I don't know about that. But I might be able to give it a shove in the right direction."

"What do you need me to do?" she asked.

"If it happens, treat me the same. Don't pity me. Don't ask me how it's going. And don't suggest things I can do to make it better."

"Okay." She nodded, then looked at the clock. It was a little after six. "So . . . uh . . . weren't we supposed to start at nine? Don't you think you jumped the gun a little?" There was a small smile on her face, but she looked worried.

"I got a little anxious," I said. I pulled the photocopy I had gotten from the library out of my back pocket. I made sure the picture on it was facing up, then placed it on the counter next to my mom. "I found something."

She gasped, short and sharp. She dropped the mug she was holding; it shattered on the tiles, splashing coffee on the floor in an amoeba-type shape. She didn't seem to notice. Her breath was coming in jagged gasps.

The picture was sixteen years old, based on the date of the newspaper. I didn't know the specific local event that it was from. It didn't say. It must have been some kind of party. My father was wearing a tuxedo. He was sitting, smiling at the camera. I had seen photos of him with a sincere smile; this wasn't it. Sitting on his lap was Roberta Carling, Kevin and Liz's mom; although she wasn't Mrs. Carling at the time. She was still Roberta Santini. Sitting next to my dad, and also wearing a tuxedo, was Albert Carling. My mom was sitting on his lap. Her smile looked as forced as my dad's. The caption read THE SANTINI SISTERS AND THEIR MEN. ROBERTA AND HER FIANCÉ, JAMES STEVENS; KATHERINE AND HER FIANCÉ, ALBERT CARLING.

There were so many things about the photo that hurt, I didn't know which to focus on. It was like getting attacked by a swarm of bees and trying to identify which one had the sharpest stinger.

"Where did you—?" she started to ask. "How—?"

"The library," I said. "As to how, there was a clue, a series of letters and numbers written on a piece of paper. They found it in the glove compartment of Dad's car."

"I remember," she whispered.

"I've spent the past few years trying to figure out what they meant. Today, I finally did. They led me to that." I pointed at the picture. It was still on the counter. My mom hadn't touched it.

She was crying pretty steadily now. My eyes were starting to tear up, too, but I couldn't lose it yet. There were things I needed to know. "You and Mrs. Carling are sisters," I said.

She nodded.

"You were engaged to Mr. Carling, and Dad was engaged to your sister."

She nodded again.

"And somewhere along the line, you and Dad jilted them and ran off together."

She let out a sob.

"So, he's my uncle, she's my aunt, and Kevin and Liz are my cousins."

She nodded again.

"And Santini's is partially yours."

She shook her head. "No. My dad—"

"My grandfather."

"Your . . . grandfather left the restaurant to Roberta when your father and I ran off."

"You left town?"

"We went to New York. Your father tried to make it as a musician. He was good, and he was starting to make headway when I got pregnant with you. But trying to make it as a musician in New York with a pregnant wife at home and no support is an uphill climb."

"So he quit, and you came back here?"

"We thought that maybe things had died down enough—"

"Or your pregnancy might soften your family up a bit."

"It didn't," she said. "My father wanted to talk to me, I think, but Roberta made him choose between us. She wanted me to suffer. She and Albert had found some sort of relationship. I'm not sure either of them would call it love, but it was something."

"So that's why Mr. Carling is so hard on you."

She wiped her eyes with her hands, then took a deep

breath. "He's not," she said. "It's all an act. If it weren't for Albert, we wouldn't be making it."

I was confused, and then another seemingly random piece clicked into place. "He owns this building, doesn't he? He's 'Big A.'"

"Big A?"

"The phone," I said. "In my office. Sometimes it rings, and when I pick it up, some guy on the other line asks for 'Big A.' When I try to take a message, he hangs up."

"Yeah, Albert owns this place. He doesn't want to take rent from us, but I make him. He gave me the job at the restaurant, over Roberta's objections, and always gives me first pick of holiday shifts. If someone calls in sick, he calls me first."

"But he acts mean to you because that's easier to explain—to his wife, to anyone that may know the story . . . to me."

"Yeah," she said. "Plus, I think Roberta really likes the idea of having me as her lowly employee . . . able to rub my nose in the dirt with the snap of her fingers."

"Does he still love you?"

She paused. "I don't know."

"Do you love him?"

She paused. "I don't know."

I took a deep breath and let it out slowly. "So what about Dad? What happened to him?'

A hardness crept across her face. Tears still fell, but they seemed like remnants of her feelings from a couple of minutes ago. "I don't know."

"Nothing?"

"No," she said. "If I did, that's not something I'd keep from you."

"You have an idea, though."

She looked down at her hands, but there was nothing in them or on them to fidget with.

"When we came back, all he talked about was leaving again. The more we stayed, the more he realized that leaving wasn't going to be easy. And everyone that we knew . . ." She wiped her mouth with her hand. "No one wanted to talk to us. Our old friends, our families . . . no one. We even got some threats."

"What?"

"The police checked them out," she said. "They turned out to be nothing. Just some idiots sticking their noses where they didn't belong."

"So, someone could have driven him off. Or hurt him, or . . ."

"Yes. Or he could have just run off," she said, in a way

that made it clear which possibility she believed. "Here's the thing, Matt, and it took me a *really* long time to make peace with this: If someone did hurt him, or worse, there's nothing I can do about it. The only thing I can do is take care of you the best I can. That's it. I can't save him, or"—she took a deep, shuddery breath—"or bring him back, if that's the case. I can't even 'find justice for him,' which always looks so easy in movies or on TV. I can't do anything like that. The best I can do is try to take care of *you*. Do you understand?"

My jaw tightened. I did, but I didn't.

"That's only because you're wired differently," my mom said, as if she had snatched my last thought out of the air. "Do you at least understand that?"

I nodded slowly. I licked my lips and forced myself to ask the last question I had left. "And if he left on his own?"

"Then screw him," my mom said, the color rising in her cheeks. "Let him stay lost."

She stepped close to me and grabbed me by the shoulders. Her face was inches from mine. The tears were gone, her eyes suddenly clear and bright . . . and hard as granite. "Your dad loved you—I'm sure he still does— but here's the thing . . . no one—NO ONE—could drive me away from you," she said. "You got that? It's not possible. If someone even tried, they'd quickly wish they hadn't."

"You're small, but you pack a wallop," I said.

"When it counts . . . yeah. And kiddo, nothing counts more to me than you."

She grabbed my head and planted a hard kiss on my cheek, then pulled me in for a hug . . . the big kind that has a little rocking-back-and-forth to it. She took a deep, sniffly breath, then pulled back and held me by the shoulders again. "You okay?"

"In some ways, yeah. In other ways . . . I'm not sure," I said. "I still have my whole case thing to worry about, so that's at least a little bit of a distraction."

"And when that's done?"

I shrugged. "I'll have a mental breakdown. But that might happen anyway when I get put in the Outs."

"So, a nice little two-for-one deal."

I nodded with mock enthusiasm. "Crazy, now at half the price!"

She laughed, then grabbed both my cheeks and pinched. "How'd you get so funny, huh?"

"Ow! All right, I'm done." I moved my face away from

her pincers. "I think I need a pizza or three," I said, and held up a twenty.

My mom shook her head, but I could tell she was impressed. "I think I chose the wrong profession," she said.

I smiled. "Yeah . . . me too."

After our discussion, we both felt drained but wired, so we zoned out to a movie. The next thing we knew, it was six A.M., and we were waking up to the TV blaring some infomercial about the life-altering power of a vegetable chopper. We peeled ourselves off the couch and started our morning routine.

I was still getting ready when Mom headed for the exit. I met her at the door. She wrapped me in a huge hug, and although she was small, I swear she had the strength of a hundred moms.

She leaned back and grabbed me by the shoulders and

held me at arm's length. She had a sly smile on her face and a mischievous gleam in her eye. "You give 'em hell," she said.

I smiled back at her. My heart raced. It's amazing what a few words of support can do.

She gave me a kiss on the forehead, then left. I watched her car back out of the driveway, and wondered how different the world would look the next time I saw her.

The phone in my office started ringing, so I ran down to get it.

"Hello?"

"Matt? It's Jimmy."

"Hey. Listen, Mac, I'm sorry about yesterday, and about dragging you into this mess . . . and a lot of other things."

"Be sorry for the other things, but not for getting me involved in this case . . . because you didn't. If there's a story, I'm there . . . Get me?"

"Yeah, I got you."

"Listen," he said, "I wasn't calling to be a guest star in some Hallmark special. Someone dropped something off at my house last night. Want to guess what?"

"A baby unicorn?"

"Nope. More interesting than that."

He told me what it was, and he was right . . . it was pretty interesting.

"So, what do you think I should do?" he asked.

"Sell some papers," I said.

I could practically feel his smile beaming over the phone line.

I checked the clock on the wall. "I have to go," I said. "See you in a few?"

"Will you?"

"Call it wishful thinking."

"Is there any way I can help?" he asked.

"No. Just get those papers out, so if I do go in the Outs, I know I'll have some company."

I hung up the phone, grabbed all the clues that pertained to the case, and shoved them in my backpack. I grabbed the duffel bag that Vinny had given me yesterday. I even grabbed the wood box. I really didn't want a souvenir from the case that put me in the Outs. Let the blackmailer have it.

When I walked out the office door, I saw what I expected to see: Cynthia, standing there waiting for me.

"Oh. What a surprise."

"Can I walk with you?" she asked.

"I don't think I can stop you," I said.

She smiled. "No, I suppose you can't."

We walked two blocks without talking. I could feel her sneak peeks at me, but I didn't return any.

"Do you know how you're going to handle this?" she asked when we were half a block from school.

"I'm going to follow directions and hope for the best. Never know who might show up, though."

"Who? You mean the blackmailer?" she asked.

I didn't answer.

"Matt? Do you know who it is?"

"We're here," I said.

The school was large and imposing no matter what time of day it was. Looking at it always filled me with such mixed feelings. It was the main source of thrills and dread in every student's life. We never wanted to be there, but we didn't want to *not* be there and miss something. Our day could go from super great to really horrible in the twitch of a finger, and living constantly on that edge made it hard to breathe sometimes . . . but it was also exhilarating.

I started up the steps. Cynthia just stood there and watched me.

"Come on if you're coming," I said without breaking stride. I heard her follow behind me.

The halls were empty, except for the early morning light, which was dusty and had the faint smell of pencil lead and glue. I walked up the stairs to the second floor. Cynthia kept pace.

"What locker was it again?" she asked, but it sounded forced and unnatural. I smiled at her, but didn't answer.

When we got to locker 416, Will was leaning against it.

"Will," I said.

"What's this all about?" he asked. He looked at Cynthia. "And what's she doing here?"

"Couldn't be helped," I said. "She has a stake in this, too."

"How do you mean?" he asked.

"You'll see," I said. "But first things first." I pulled the manila envelope out of my bag and held it up.

His eyes went wide. A couple of beads of sweat formed on his forehead. "What—?"

"Go ahead. Take a look," I said, holding out the envelope to him. "It might jog your memory."

"Where did you get that?" His eyes kept darting from

the envelope to me, and back to the envelope. He licked his lips four times in a row. Other than that, he was hiding his anxiety well.

"The envelope?" I asked. "A basic office supply store."

His mouth tightened into a grimace. "No. The—Whatever's inside."

"You still haven't checked it," I said, practically pushing it into his chest. "I don't want there to be any misunderstanding. You know: I'm talking about one thing, and you think I'm talking about something else. Then our whole lives become like a bad sitcom."

"I—" he said, then stopped. He turned his head away from me.

I pulled the photo out of the envelope and held it up. Cynthia took a long look and gasped. I thought Will was going to grab it and crumple it up, but instead he just stood there, looking panicked. His head jerked around, scanning the hallway. Cynthia and I were the only witnesses.

I understood why he was so tense. The picture was grainy, but there was no mistaking what was going on. Two boys were standing in a locker room. One was obviously Will, even though his face wasn't clear. His size, posture, and the big number 4 on his official Franklin Middle

School basketball jersey gave it away. The other kid in the picture was Vinny Biggs. Will was holding his hand out to Vinny; Vinny was about to put something in that empty hand. Even with the graininess, you could tell it was a wad of cash.

Will stared down at his shoes. "I made that mistake a long time ago."

"Yeah, I know. The date stamp in the bottom right corner tells me that. You want to know what else that date stamp tells me? It tells me that this picture was taken the day of the Carver game. You know, the game that Pete supposedly threw."

"Date could be faked," Will mumbled.

"Yeah, it could be. One look at you tells me it wasn't, though."

Will continued to stare at his shoes. He looked miserable.

"Pete forgot to take his phone out of his shorts," he said. "He ran back to put it in his locker. On the way, he saw me talking to Vinny and decided to take a picture of us. Why? I'm not even sure he knows."

"So Pete tried to win that game on his own," I said. "That's why he wouldn't pass to you. He knew he would probably lose anyway, but he figured he'd go down swinging. Ironically, it was his fight that made it look like *he* was the one tanking . . . and that played right into your hands, didn't it?"

Will bowed his head.

"And you let him take the blame," I said.

"He wanted to take it. He offered," he said. "I didn't want to throw my whole life away just because I needed a little cash. Pete already had a Pixy Stix addiction. He was bound to mess up sooner or later. Why do you think he kept this a secret for so long?"

"Because he didn't want to rat out his friend. And he didn't think anyone would believe him, picture or no picture."

"It was more than that! Honest! The pressure was getting to him. He didn't want to play basketball anymore. All he wanted to do was get Stixed all the time."

"So instead of getting him help, you turned him into the most hated kid in school. Pete was drowning in a sea of sugar, and you tossed him an iron doughnut."

"Neither one of us realized how bad it would get for him!"

I swallowed my anger. "You know what?" I said. "I don't even care. What's done is done, right?"

The weakness and desperation drained from his face, replaced by suspicion . . . and familiarity. "Right," he said cautiously.

"Past is past," I said. "Let's talk about the future."

"What about it?"

"Well, the future—more specifically, *my* future—looks like it's going to be unpleasant," I said, "and I think it's my responsibility to myself to cushion the fall a bit. Don't you?"

He didn't say anything but gave me a look of someone with experience in these types of discussions, a look that said, *What do you want from me?*

"Here's what's going to happen," I said, unzipping the bag. "I'm going to count this money and make sure it's all there." I took out one of the money stacks and pocketed it. I zipped the bag back up and put it in the locker. "Yup, all there."

Cynthia grabbed my shoulder. "Matt? What are you doing?"

"You can't just take that!" Will said. "What about the blackmailers? They'll release my—"

"Photo?" I said. "No, they won't. If they do that, the gravy train pulls out of the station, never to return. As long as the photo stays hidden, they have a steady income. Oh, they might be miffed that the take is less than it should be, but that's not your problem. That's between them and Vinny, right? All you have to do is keep your mouth shut. Both of you."

"Matt?!?" Cynthia said. "What're you . . . ? You can't—"

"Quiet," I said. "I'm trying to *work*, here."

She looked confused, but she stopped talking. And was that a glimmer of realization I saw on her face?

"So, you're blackmailing me, too," Will said. He scowled. He bit his lip. He banged his fist on the locker four times. "You're a real jerk, you know that?"

I shrugged. "You're not exactly an angel yourself, so excuse me if I take that with a grain of salt. And what are you getting so bent out of shape for? All you have to do is not say anything. It's not like this is your money." I paused. "Is it?"

He twitched.

I smiled. "Well," I said, "not as cool off the court as you are on, are you?"

"*You're* blackmailing *me*," he said, trying to change the topic back to one in which he was the hero.

"Really? Or are you upset that I'm cutting into your profits? Maybe I should put it back then." I turned away from him, to face the locker. I opened the door and reached for the bag. Before I could grab it, I heard Cynthia gasp. I had a hunch why.

"Turn around," Will said.

I did. Will was holding a small blue squirt gun, the kind that's easy to conceal. It was pointed at me. For some reason, I couldn't stop smiling.

"You weren't blackmailing me just now, were you?" he asked. "You already knew."

I pulled out the two ransom notes and held them up. "You wrote these."

He shrugged, a smug smile uglying up his handsome face.

"You couldn't see them on the originals," I said. "They were too faint. But something happens with a photocopy sometimes, where it picks up a little indentation or a little mark that would otherwise be completely hidden. There are four little pen marks on this note, where you tapped the paper. Four . . . your lucky number. You don't do anything until you tap it four times."

"Uh-huh," Will said. "Keep going."

Cynthia's eyes kept darting from me to Will and back again.

"Pete's main connection for Stix was the Thompson twins. He had worked up a massive debt to them, and they were no longer supplying him. So Pete tried to square up with them by showing them your picture. He hoped he could lead them on, promise to give them the picture, or a copy, for a constant supply of Stix. The Thompsons agreed, then planned to take the picture by force, and use it to blackmail Vinny. If kids still thought the fix was in after all this time, it would put a major dent in Vinny's gambling operation. After Pete came down from his sugar high, he realized what he'd done by telling the Thompsons, and he assumed that the slimy little jerks would come after him. He freaked out and regretted it. He gave you the box with the photo to hold. You heard through a few connections of your own that Pete had floated your picture out there."

"You're serious, Matt?" Cynthia asked.

"Yeah . . . Will saw an opportunity . . . the Thompsons wanted to blackmail Vinny, but what if he got there first? Since Will was in the photo, Vinny would have a hard time suspecting him, especially if the photo was out in the wild. So he played a little shell game with it. He gave it to Melissa, sent a note to the Thompsons tipping them off, so they'd get their hands on it, then schemed to have someone—either me or Vinny—take it away from them. The more people who touched the box, the harder it would be to remember that Will had it in the first place. The only person who might suspect something was up was Pete. All Will had to do was play dumb with him."

"But what if the Thompsons opened the box and took the photo?" Cynthia asked.

"It wasn't even in there at that point. It didn't need to be. The *promise* of the photo was enough to have people fighting over it. Once I found the box, it was time to send out the demand notes and make it seem like there was now a third party involved."

"And you based this whole theory on four small dots on the bottom of two pieces of paper?" Will asked, that same smug smile on his face.

"Well, the ransom consisted of two hundred and fifty-six dollars, which is four to the fourth power," I said, "and four boxes of candy. Also, I never said the dots were on the bottom of the ransom notes."

"Yes, you did."

"No, he didn't," Cynthia said.

Will started laughing. "Looks like you got me again. You are impressive, Matt."

"Thanks," I said sarcastically. "That means a lot coming from you."

"It should. I know a little something about being the best, so I appreciate it when I see it in others."

"Well, at least you're humble about it," I said.

"Why?" Cynthia asked him. "Why would you do that? To Melissa? To the school?"

Will laughed again, but there was no humor in it; it sounded bitter and sad. "Look at me. Do you see this shirt? Do you know how expensive it is? Or these shoes?"

"You're kidding, right?" Cynthia said. "You betrayed the school's trust and ruined a girl's life because of your fashion sense?"

"Who am I?" he yelled. "Huh? Am I Will Atkins, average middle school student? Can I come to school in generic pants and an old shirt?"

"Yes!"

"No. You may know a little about what it's like to be watched by everyone, every day . . . but you have no idea what it's like to be everyone's hero. Kids idolize me!"

"Quite an ego you've got there," Cynthia said.

"Tell me it's not true," he said. "Go ahead."

We didn't say anything.

"That's right," he said. "Because you know I'm right. I have an image to uphold. And everyone—EVERYONE— including the teachers, wants me to live up to that image." He moved his hands up and down in front of himself, like a model on a game show presenting potential prizes. "This is the image that everyone wants. And I have to give it to them. I mean, what choice do I have?"

"Your clothes don't matter," I said. "Kids look up to *you*."

"Ha!" he said. "Right. Because kids around here are soooo thoughtful and understanding. You saw what they did to my girlfriend."

"YOU did that to her," Cynthia yelled.

"No!" he yelled back. "NO! I had her splashed with water. That's it! The kids in this school . . . THEY did the rest. And you honestly believe that if I came to school in the clothes my parents could actually afford, they wouldn't turn on me? Start ridiculing me? Huh?"

"But I've been to your house," Cynthia said. "You're not—"

"Poor? No. We're 'middle class,'" he said. "Middle

class. Ha! What a joke. Why don't you ask me how long it's been since my dad had a job? Huh? No, nobody cares about that. I'm Will, the hero who always puts this school first. I'm the savior of this rotten school!"

"Savior?!?" Cynthia yelled. "You're the one who's ruining it!"

"That's not the story around here," he sneered. "The story I'm going to tell is that I'm the hero, and you two are just a couple of cheap thugs trying to blackmail me." He lifted the squirt gun, aiming it between us, so we couldn't tell which one of us he was going to soak first. "But I stood my ground and didn't let you win. The idiots around here are going to eat it up."

"You do realize you're being double-crossed, right?" I asked.

His sneer faded. "What do you mean?"

"Your partner," I said. "He's double-crossing you."

"*Pff!* Yeah, right! What partner?"

"Someone just dropped off a copy of the photo at the newspaper this morning," I said. "It's running in a special edition. In fact, it's being printed right now, as we speak."

"Pete! That no good, little—"

"Save it," I said. "It wasn't him. He gave me the phone

with the original picture on it, knowing that Jimmy Mac would have to help me blow it up just to see what was in it. So Pete already knew that Jimmy had a copy of the photo. Why would he waste his time sending it to him again? He wouldn't. The person who sent that photo to the paper this morning was the only other person to have it, the only other person who might want to see it in print. He used you to get it and make a little money, but now he's cutting his ties with you. Isn't that right, Kevin?"

Kevin stepped out from around the corner, a big green squirt gun in his hand. Liz was standing next to him. "Yeah, that about sums it up. You want to finish explaining it to Will? He looks a little lost."

I stared at them. Liz wouldn't look at me. Her gaze was fixed on the floor a few feet in front of her. I felt Cynthia's hand on my shoulder.

"You know what?" Kevin said. "Looks like you need a moment to let this all sink in, Matt, so I'll explain it."

"You set me up?" Will asked.

"Sure," Kevin said. "Haven't you ever played chess?" He shot me a malicious look and smiled. Liz didn't move.

"What the hell are you talking about?" Will yelled.

"Look, Will," he continued, "you're a powerful piece . . . maybe even a rook . . . but you're still expendable."

"Kevin—and his sister—have a bigger target than a few blackmail bucks and some candy," I said.

"That's right. I told you I was leaving Vinny's crew, Matt," Kevin said. "I just didn't tell you it was because I was taking over."

"Yeah, I worked that part out all on my own."

"What gave it away?"

"The Katie hit," I replied. "Everything you did up to that point had a business reason. Putting Katie in the Outs didn't. It was personal."

"Damn straight it was," he said.

"Was it personal for you too, Liz?" I asked.

Liz still wouldn't look at me.

"Don't worry about her," Kevin said. "Worry about me."

I glared at Liz for a moment longer. "Fine. The other thing was that little present you left for me in the 'decorative' box."

Kevin laughed, but it was cold and full of hurt. "I'm so glad you figured that out, Matt. I was beginning to lose faith in you as a detective."

"What the hell is going on here?" Will yelled. "What about our deal?"

Kevin turned on him. "It's simple. You thought I was just trying to make some money, maybe even show that Vinny was weak because he was getting blackmailed. I'll admit that was part of it. I was hoping that there would be a bit of an uprising when it was revealed that Vinny had cheated to win money on that game, and all the kids who lost would rise up and take him out . . . maybe it'll still happen. We'll see when the paper comes out."

"That paper isn't coming out."

We all turned to see Vinny and his crew of thugs. One of them was holding Jimmy Mac in his man-size hand. He only needed one. Jenny was standing directly behind Vinny; she was holding a squirt gun pointed directly at the front of Liz's skirt.

"Vinny," Kevin said. "So glad you could join us."

"Getting a little crowded in the hallway," I said. "Maybe I should go."

"Stick around, Matt," Kevin said. "I still have a surprise for you."

"Can't wait."

Vinny's goons raised their giant soakers and pointed

them in Kevin's direction. For the moment, Cynthia and I were forgotten. "So," Vinny said to Kevin, "it's come to this."

Kevin smiled. "I know you've known for a while."

"I've suspected for a while, but I didn't know," Vinny said. "I guess I like to imagine my employees are more loyal than they actually are." He sighed.

"You've had a good run," Kevin said. "Time for someone else."

"Who? You? Please . . . You have some smarts and savvy, Carling, I'll give you that, but you think you know more than you do. You have no idea how to run an organization as broad as mine."

"You don't think?" Kevin said. Almost as if on cue, we were suddenly surrounded by kids. They all had giant soakers, too. I recognized a lot of them as kids who were part of Vinny's crew. It looked like they had decided that Kevin was the wave of the future.

"Huh," Vinny said. "Seems I've underestimated you."

"Tell me something I don't know," Kevin responded.

Vinny cracked his knuckles. "You know I'm not going to let you just move in."

"I wouldn't want it if you weren't going to fight for it."

Kevin moved his head from side to side, cracking his neck.

"Everybody freeze!" Will shouted. He had his little blue squirt gun in his hand. He was completely panicked, not pointing at anyone specifically . . . more just waving it around.

Vinny looked bored. Kevin looked amused.

"I almost forgot you were still here," Kevin said to him. "Sorry, Will, but I don't think I'm going to be able to back you up anymore. You might want to think about dropping that and walking out of here."

"You set me up!" Will yelled at Kevin. "I'm supposed to trust you now?"

Vinny smiled. "Looks like he didn't give you a choice."

"No, you fat little twerp! You're the one without a choice! I'm the hero in this school! I'm the capta—!" A burst of water came from behind Vinny, catching Will square in the front of his pants.

"Shut up!" Jenny cackled, water still dripping from her freshly fired Super Soaker.

The wet spot started spreading on Will's pants. He shrieked.

"You're next, Matty-boy!" Jenny said, walking toward me, pumping her soaker.

I cocked my fists, ready to go down swinging. Before I could move, Cynthia stepped forward. "Hey, sweetheart!" she said, then punched Jenny square in the nose.

"Gahh!" Jenny yelled. She went down hard, blood pouring out of her nose, her soaker clattering to the floor, forgotten.

And that's when all hell broke loose.

Water blasted everywhere. Everyone scattered. I hit the floor and started crawling. Two of Vinny's guards went down screaming. Vinny was splashed, but the water caught him too high to do any good. His remaining guards formed a barrier around him. They blasted the hallway, providing cover for Vinny to escape.

I was on the floor, looking for Cynthia, but found Kevin instead. It might've been more accurate to say that Kevin found me. He grabbed me by the collar and turned me over on my back. I looked up at him. "Congratulations," I said. "You fooled me. I thought you had a heart instead of a money-filled hole in your chest. I thought—"

"What? That we were going to be friends again?" He laughed. It sounded like a metal pick being dragged across a chalkboard.

"So you're just a complete jerk, then? Is that it?"

"Oh, Matt . . . you think you can get under my skin? You really have no idea, do you?"

"I do now, cousin. Is it because your mommy doesn't love you? Or because your daddy doesn't love your mommy?"

I had found Kevin's button. He dropped the squirt gun. He didn't want humiliation for me anymore; he wanted pain. He picked me up off the floor, then threw me across the hallway like a cheap rubber ball.

"Your crappy parents are the reason that my family is miserable," he said, striding toward me. He picked me up again, but this time he punched me in the stomach. The pain was so sharp, I almost threw up on his shoes. He held me upright. "I wanted you to know why we'd never be friends again!" he yelled into my face. "Never!" He reared back to punch me again.

"Back off!" came a voice from behind me. Kevin looked up. After catching my breath, I turned around. Cynthia was holding Jenny's Super Soaker, aimed at Kevin. "Now!"

"And if I don't?" Kevin asked.

Cynthia pumped the soaker as an answer.

Kevin did as he was told, letting me drop back to the floor.

"Matt . . . are you okay?" Cynthia asked.

"I don't know," I said.

"Hi, Cynthia," Kevin said, smiling. "I'm not sure we've met. I'm Kevin Carling."

"Shut up, Kevin Carling," Cynthia said. "I'm taking you in."

Kevin smiled. "Taking me in? That sounds like hall monitor talk. But *you're* not a hall monitor, are you?"

Cynthia didn't say anything. She gave me a quick, guilty glance. It was the only answer she needed to give.

"Oooh!" Kevin squealed. "You ARE a hall monitor! And undercover this whole time! Does lover boy know you've been playing him?"

"Yeah," I said. "I knew."

A small smile passed over Cynthia's face, as if I had just passed another one of her tests.

Kevin's smile didn't disappear, but it hardened. "It's a shame," he said. "You're so pretty."

"What?" she asked.

"Cynthia!" I yelled. "Get down!"

I was too late. The blast came from the right, and caught her mostly on the left leg. Not a full frontal shot, but still effective. She fell backward, firing her soaker harmlessly at the ceiling.

Liz stood there, water dripping from the barrel of her soaker. Her face was frozen in a blank expression. It looked like she was in shock.

The door to the school opened, and kids started pouring in from the outside.

"Come on!" Kevin yelled into Liz's face, but she didn't seem to hear him. He grabbed her arm and dragged her off down the hall.

I ran over to Cynthia. She was lying on the floor, breathing heavily. Kids were starting to run over, crowding around her, cutting her off from escape. Jimmy Mac was trying to run over, too, but he couldn't get through the crowd.

"PEE-PEE PANTS! PEE-PEE PANTS!" they yelled.

"Matt?" Cynthia whispered.

"It's okay . . . I'm right here . . ." I cradled her head in my lap.

"I didn't do too hot."

"You did great," I said.

"Katie put me up to it. She . . . she knew you wouldn't let her help you—"

"So she sent you."

"You saved her sister. She was in your debt. She respected you, Matt . . . more than you know."

"PEE-PEE PANTS! PEE-PEE PANTS!" The chants from the crowd were getting louder as more kids streamed into the school.

She smiled weakly. "She told me I would fall for you . . . Melanie said the same thing . . . They were right . . ." She started to cry.

"PEE-PEE PANTS! PEE-PEE PANTS!"

"Shut up!" I yelled. I stood up and pushed the kid closest to me.

"PEE-PEE PANTS! PEE-PEE PANTS!"

Two big kids grabbed me by the front of my shirt and pulled me into the crowd. "No!" I yelled. "Cynthia!" A punch hit me in the stomach. Another hit me in the jaw. I tried to hit back, but it was like trying to punch the ocean.

"Leave me alone!" Cynthia screamed. She stood up, then ran down the hallway, pushing her way through the pack of chanting kids.

Jimmy Mac ran after her. Some other kids started following her, too, but after a little while they gave up. Then the bell rang, and kids filtered into their classrooms, as if nothing had happened.

I sat down on the floor, trying my hardest to get my head together, but it wasn't happening. I felt like I had just been in a flash blizzard that left twenty inches, then disappeared without a trace. I was dizzy. Everyone I cared about was either gone or trying to destroy me. And to top it all off, I was late for homeroom.

I thought about standing up but didn't. I just sat there in the middle of the hall, trying to think of my next move, and wondering when I should make it.

23

I saw her leave school around 12:30, right after her lunch period. I knew she was going to skip out. After everything that happened, I was surprised she waited as long as she did. Fifteen minutes later, I managed to do the same.

The weather had changed since the morning. The temperature had dropped 20 degrees and the sky was blanketed with gray clouds. It looked like a kindergartner had made the sky for an art project, using the cotton stuffing from an old quilt. I zipped up my jacket, shoved my hands in my pockets, and walked.

The rest of the morning had been a perfect example of revenge-fueled chaos. Word had spread quickly about Will, then spread even wider once Jimmy Mac got his paper out. After his pants got soaked, Will had escaped the Outs by hiding in the locker room, but the kids in school weren't going to let him off that easily. Outs or no Outs, Will's popularity had taken a direct nuclear blast. Kids had trusted him. He had been their symbol of hope. And he turned out to be a sham . . . The kids felt like suckers, and they wanted to make Will pay.

The coach made an official announcement before lunch: Will's basketball career was over, at least at the Frank. Who knows if the high school coaches would feel differently. Will still had talent. Sometimes that was enough to get you a second chance. But here's the funny thing: Being the tallest kid in middle school doesn't mean squat over there. High school is a much bigger pond, and not only are some of the fish bigger, some of them can actually dunk.

I thought about Cynthia, about how the kids attacked her in the hall. They put her in the Outs without a second thought, even though she hadn't done a damn thing to any of them. Cynthia . . . beautiful Cynthia. Her mom had to come and pick her up. I snuck out of second period to watch her go. She leaned on her mother for support, her toughness gone. Another amazing person snuffed out by the Outs.

I shivered a little and zipped up my coat even farther. I picked up the pace.

I walked past the downtown area, over to the boardwalk that ran along the river. Liz was standing with her back to me, facing the water. I knew she would be. It was her favorite place in town, the place she went when she was trying to figure out a problem. I walked up alongside her. She didn't react, as if she had known all along that I'd be coming.

"Liz," I said.

"Matt."

"Or should we call each other . . . well, what's short for 'cousin'? 'Coz'?"

She didn't answer.

"Interesting morning, huh, coz?" I asked.

She sniffled. I couldn't tell if it was from the cold or from something else. "Did you walk all this way to ask me that?" she asked.

"I came for the view. Consider my observation about the morning a bonus."

"What do you want, Matt?"

"Don't you think you're directing your anger at the wrong person?" I said.

She turned and looked at me. Her eyes were bloodshot; her mouth was pulled into a sharp little frown that meant she was really angry or had been crying. "This is your fault."

"My fault," I repeated, calmly.

"You're the one who let this happen. You're the reason it's gone this far. You're why I can't—" She started crying. "Your fault," she repeated.

Even though I was angry at her, I wanted to forget this whole stupid system we had to live by . . . just forget everything that came before this moment . . . and pull her into my arms. Hug her. Tell her everything was going to be okay. But I didn't . . . I couldn't. Maybe if we were still in ellie, where life was simpler, and the problems black and white. But this was middle school, and there were no easy answers.

"My fault," I said again. "Amazing. My memory must be really messed up, because I was pretty sure it was *you*, coz, pulling the trigger on that soaker this morning. You do remember putting a girl in the Outs, don't you?"

Tears rolled down her cheeks. "I remember," she said, barely above a whisper.

"So tell me how this is *my* fault."

"Because you could stop this . . . this whole Outs crap. You could end it."

"Me."

"Yes. You."

"Really? What other powers do I have?" I asked. "Oooh! Can I fly? Can I cure the common cold?"

"And that's why you won't," she said. "Because whenever someone challenges you to actually *do* something, you create a fortress of sarcasm and bullcrap, and then go hide in it."

"You're totally right," I said. "This entire week I did absolutely nothing! Oh, and *your* way is MUCH better. Look how well it worked out! Your plan put three kids in the Outs and started a war between two power-hungry bullies . . . a war that could drag the whole school down."

"No . . . no, that's not what I was doing. "

"You're kidding, right? I don't know what you *thought* you were doing, but you'd better check in with your brother, because I think he's working with a different game plan."

"It doesn't matter," she said. "*He* doesn't matter."

"It sure looked like he mattered this morning."

"Forget it," she said. "I thought, of all people, *you* might understand, but . . . forget it."

"Yeah, I understand all right. Little chess queen thinks that the whole school is her game board, and she's going to win."

"No! It's not—"

"What are you trying to win, chess queen? Huh? Money? Power?"

"Stop it, Matt! Stop!"

I turned toward her. "Look at me."

"No, Matt . . . I—"

"Look at me!" I yelled. She turned and looked at me, squinting as if my face were a bright light, hurting her eyes. "How did it make you feel to pull that trigger?" I yelled. "Huh? How did it make you feel? Powerful?"

"Stop, Matt . . . ," she said, sobbing. "Please . . ."

"Did it make you feel powerful to ruin that girl's life?"

"NO!" she screamed. "No! It made me feel horrible! I can't stop seeing the look on her face . . . I . . . I can't stop crying . . . I . . ." Her words dissolved into incoherent crying sounds. But then she closed her eyes and took a deep breath. She let it out slowly, then opened her eyes. "I've chosen my path," she said calmly. "I'm taking it all the way to the end."

"And what's the end for you?"

"You'll find out."

"I already know," I said. My anger faded. I looked at her and smiled.

She looked at me with a mixture of confusion, suspicion, and disbelief. "No, you don't."

I turned away from her and stared out over the water. "Strong current," I said.

She wasn't sure what I was getting at, but she stopped and listened.

"Even a strong swimmer would have a problem keeping his head above water in a current that powerful," I continued. "Don't you think?"

I saw her nod out of the corner of my eye.

"And even if you were a strong swimmer, you'd have to be really foolish to jump in without a really good reason," I said. "But if there *was* a good reason for you to jump in—say, a bag full of mostly innocent kittens that needed saving—you'd want to make sure you were swimming in the right direction, right?"

She nodded again.

"Because if you didn't, then you *and* the kittens would drown, right?"

"I won't let you drown," she said. "I knew you'd figure it out."

"The Katie hit gave it away," I said. "At first I thought it was personal. Your brother did, too . . . still does, I bet. But it wasn't . . . was it?"

"No."

"Katie Kondo, Nikki Fingers, Cynthia Shea . . . plus a bunch of big kids who used to be bullies. That's a formidable force. And that's not even counting the soon-to-be casualties from this war you engineered. Hit kids from both sides are going to get popped. The Outs are going to start growing exponentially. Pretty soon, both sides are going to start running out of soldiers. And as their armies shrink—"

"The Outs' army grows."

"Quite a plan, coz," I said.

"And you knew this the whole time?" she asked.

"The whole time I was here talking to you? Yeah."

"So . . . what? You just wanted to see me cry?"

"Kind of," I said. "These aren't game pieces you're

dealing with. These are kids . . . real kids . . . and wiping them off the game board, even though it's for 'the greater good,' is going to hurt them. And that hurt is going to change them, some for the better, some for the worse. I wanted to make sure you knew it."

"You're thinking about her," Liz said. "About Cynthia."

"Yeah." No sense in lying.

"You liked her?"

"Sure," I said, "but not in the way you think."

"How do you know what I think?"

"Lucky guess, or wishful thinking . . . you decide. Anyway, Cynthia was interesting, surprising . . ."

"Gorgeous."

I shrugged. "That was the least interesting thing about her," I said.

Liz was quiet for a second. "So I guess I made the right call . . . you know, ending things between us."

"I guess. Plus, you and I are cousins, right? Kinda weird . . ."

"Right . . . weird . . ."

"So, what's the next step in your master plan, O Grand Chess Master?" I asked.

"They need a leader," she said. "Katie's close."

"But not close enough."

Liz shook her head. "She wants to bulldoze right through the Outs, but the others won't follow her. They fear and respect her, but they don't trust her."

"Yeah. She busted some of those kids. They're probably not sure she'll have their back when it all goes down."

"It's more than that," she said. "She doesn't inspire them. And if she can't inspire them . . . ALL of them . . ."

"Then the revolution is over before it even gets started."

"The kids in the Frank will bury her, and no one will want to try it ever again."

"So?" I asked.

"So, whoever's going to pull it off would have one shot. They'd have to be crazy, smart, charismatic, savvy—"

"Why don't you just ask me?" I said.

"Look who has a high opinion of himself."

"But a low sense of self-preservation . . ."

"Vinny and Kevin are both gunning for you now," she said. "What do you have to lose?"

"Oh, you mean besides everything?"

"Not everything," she said.

"Yeah, I guess I'll always have family. Is that what you mean, coz?"

"Yeah, about that whole 'coz' thing . . . ," she said, and smiled. "I'm adopted."

I stared at her.

"Some detective you are," she said, as she grabbed my hand.

Her look of triumph changed to one of confusion when her fingers felt the small piece of paper that I was holding. I smiled at her. She took it and unfolded it. It was a photocopy of a newspaper clipping, one of the two that I had gotten at the library that day. This one was a small story that had been buried in a later issue of the paper, about how Albert Carling had adopted the infant daughter of two out-of-town friends who had been killed in a car accident in New York City.

She looked down at the article and smiled. She didn't read it. I had a hunch she had seen it before. "Well . . ."

"After I found out the truth about my parents," I said, "I went looking for other stories, to see what else had been hidden from me. I thought that one was particularly interesting."

She took my hand again.

"Not bad," she said.

"I have my moments."

"So, it looks like our lives just got a little . . . complicated."

"Mine's always been complex," I said. "You're just catching up."

She smiled and leaned her head against my shoulder. We stood there for a minute, listening to the water as it lapped against the posts of the dock.

"This is going to take some planning," she said.

"Yeah. Know anyone who's good at that?"

She looked up at me, her head still on my shoulder. "Will you stick with me?" she asked.

"To the end," I said.

We held each other, and listened to the water.

Acknowledgments

To my agent, Stephen Barbara, for his patience, support, and DYJ attitude.

To my editor, Susan Van Metre, for her patience, kindness, and exceptional judgment.

To my film agent, Jason Dravis, for his patience and understanding.

To my mom, dad, sister, Nonnie, and the rest of my family, for their patience, support, and love.

To Steve & Sarah, Melissa & Peter, Joe, John & Mel, Bill, and the rest of my friends, for their patience and true friendship.

To my wife, Teryse, for her patience and unconditional love.

To Emily and Matthew, for their patience and joy, their innocence and unpredictability.

And lastly, to Bobby Grether . . . You may not remember, but you stood up for me when I was unwilling or unable to stand up for myself. I wish every kid who had to face bullies had someone like you to watch out for them. Thank you.